"This isn't so bad, is it?" Josh asked eventually, his voice low.

"What?" Ashley murmured.

"Being here, with me, just existing in the moment."

She smiled. "No," she admitted, filled with wonder at just how right it felt. "It's not bad at all."

"Then why would you give it up one second before you have to?" he asked.

Good question, she thought, right before she snuggled more tightly against him. Why give up something that felt this right? She'd eventually have to think about that, worry it to death, in all probability. But not right now. In fact, it could wait till later.

She sighed happily. Much, much later.

Dear Reader,

We're deep into spring, and the season and romance always seem synonymous to me. So why not let your reading reflect that? Start with Sherryl Woods's next book in THE ROSE COTTAGE SISTERS miniseries, *The Laws of Attraction.* This time it's Ashley's turn to find love at the cottage—which the hotshot attorney promptly does, with a man who appears totally different from the cutthroat lawyers she usually associates with. But you know what they say about appearances....

Karen Rose Smith's *Cabin Fever* is the next book in our MONTANA MAVERICKS: GOLD RUSH GROOMS continuity, in which a handsome playboy and his beautiful secretary are hired to investigate the mine ownership issue. But they're snowbound in a cabin...and work can only kill so much time! And in *Lori's Little Secret* by Christine Rimmer, the next of her BRAVO FAMILY TIES stories, a young woman who was always the shy twin has a big secret (two, actually): seven years ago she pretended to be her more outgoing sister—which resulted in a night of passion and a baby, now child. And said child's father is back in town... Judy Duarte offers another of her BAYSIDE BACHELORS, in *Worth Fighting For,* in which a single adoptive mother—with the help of her handsome neighbor, who's dealing with a loss of his own—grapples with the possibility of losing her child. In Elizabeth Harbison's hilarious new novel, a young woman who wonders how to get her man finds help in a book entitled, well, *How To Get Your Man.* But she's a bit confused about which man she really wants to get! And in *His Baby to Love* by Karen Sandler, a long-recovered alcoholic needs to deal with her unexpected pregnancy, so she gratefully accepts her friend's offer of her chalet for the weekend. But she gets an unexpected roommate—the one man who'd pointed her toward recovery...and now has some recovering of his own to do.

So enjoy, and we'll see you next month, when things once again start to heat up, in Silhouette Special Edition!

Sincerely yours,

Gail Chasan
Senior Editor

SHERRYL WOODS

The Laws of Attraction

Silhouette®
SPECIAL EDITION®
Published by Silhouette Books
America's Publisher of Contemporary Romance

SILHOUETTE BOOKS

ISBN 0-373-24681-1

THE LAWS OF ATTRACTION

This edition published by arrangement with Harlequin Books S.A.

Visit Silhouette Books at www.eHarlequin.com

Printed in U.S.A.

Books by Sherryl Woods

Silhouette Special Edition

Vows

Love #769
Honor #775
Cherish #781
Kate's Vow #823
A Daring Vow #855
A Vow To Love #885

And Baby Makes Three

A Christmas Blessing #1001
Natural Born Daddy #1007
The Cowboy and His Baby #1009
The Rancher and His Unexpected Daughter #1016

The Bridal Path

A Ranch for Sara #1083
Ashley's Rebel #1087
Danielle's Daddy Factor #1094

And Baby Makes Three: The Next Generation

The Littlest Angel #1142
Natural Born Trouble #1156
Unexpected Mommy #1171
The Cowgirl and the Unexpected Wedding #1208
Natural Born Lawman #1216
The Cowboy and His Wayward Bride #1234
Suddenly, Annie's Father #1268

The Calamity Janes

Do You Take This Rebel? #1394
Courting the Enemy #1411
To Catch a Thief #1418
Wrangling the Redhead #1429

And Baby Makes Three: The Delacourts of Texas

The Cowboy and the New Year's Baby #1291
Dylan and the Baby Doctor #1309
The Pint-Sized Secret #1333
Marrying a Delacourt #1352
The Delacourt Scandal #1363

The Devaneys

Ryan's Place #1489
Sean's Reckoning #1495
Michael's Discovery #1513
Patrick's Destiny #1549
Daniel's Desire #1555

Million Dollar Destinies

Isn't It Rich? #1597
Priceless #1603
Treasured #1609

The Rose Cottage Sisters

Three Down the Aisle #1663
What's Cooking? #1675
The Laws of Attraction #1681

Silhouette Books

Silhouette Summer Sizzlers 1990
"A Bridge to Dreams"

Maternity Leave 1998
"The Paternity Test"

So This Is Christmas 2002
"The Perfect Holiday"

The Unclaimed Baby
The Calamity Janes

SHERRYL WOODS

has written more than seventy-five novels. She also operates her own bookstore, Potomac Sunrise, in Colonial Beach, Virginia. If you can't visit Sherryl at her store, then be sure to drop her a note at P.O. Box 490326, Key Biscayne, FL 33149 or check out her Web site at www.sherrylwoods.com.

Dear Reader,

Just the thought of retreating to the isolation of Rose Cottage is enough to give high-powered attorney Ashley D'Angelo hives, but when her professional life unravels, her sisters insist it's the only place she belongs.

Despite the family track record, which is two for two in finding love matches at Rose Cottage, the last thing Ashley expects while she's sitting around nursing her injured pride is to find love.

But if Ashley is skeptical about the whole serenity and love thing, Josh Madison is the exact opposite. He's craving the peace and quiet and slower lifestyle, and he has a thing or two to teach Ashley about relaxation.

Yes, indeed, Josh has a very deft touch, and Rose Cottage does it again. Wouldn't you think a brilliant woman like Ashley would have seen it coming? Sometimes there's just no way around magic.

All best,

Sherryl Woods

Prologue

The headline said it all: Guilty Man Freed.

Albert "Tiny" Slocum was a charming two-bit punk who'd hoodwinked his lawyer and an entire jury into believing in his innocence. It hadn't helped that the case presented against him hadn't been airtight. He walked out of the courtroom a free man with a clean slate, thanks to Ashley D'Angelo, who'd once been dubbed Boston's "savior of the innocent."

Of course, Tiny had spoiled his innocent act a bit when he'd had the audacity to turn to the jury in front of the judge and call them all suckers. That moment of pure cockiness had proved just what a psychopath he was. It had also earned him a promise from the prosecutor that he would find a way to put Tiny right back behind bars, maybe not for the crime of killing Letitia

Baldwin for which he'd just been acquitted, but for some other heinous act he had already committed. There were bound to be some.

That appalling scene had also been the moment that every criminal defense attorney with a conscience dreaded. Ashley D'Angelo was no exception.

Ashley hadn't much liked three-hundred-pound Tiny, but she *had* believed in him. He'd declared his innocence with such passion. He had a clever mind and a sharp wit that he'd used effectively to charm her into thinking he couldn't possibly be guilty of such a barbaric crime. In the course of what appeared to have started as a botched purse-snatching, elderly, frail Letitia Baldwin had been beaten nearly to death by someone in an obvious rage at finding only a few dollars in her wallet. Tiny had professed to love and respect women. His own mother had backed him up, saying he was the ideal son. Ashley, who'd built her entire reputation on defending the innocent, had been taken in.

She'd also seen all the holes in the prosecution's case. She'd spent months building a defense, but before she could spend a single second feeling triumphant over the not-guilty verdict, she'd been hit with the gut-wrenching realization that Tiny was indeed responsible for Letitia Baldwin's massive injuries. The elderly woman had later died in the emergency room, changing the charge from assault to murder.

There wasn't enough merlot in all the wine cellars in Boston to help Ashley get over that sickening image. The crime scene photos played over and over in her head, like a looping newsreel that never quit.

Later, in the dark of night, when she was lying sleepless in her fancy penthouse apartment, Ashley had finally admitted that on some level she'd known all along that she was defending a murderer—and doing it with the kind of aggressive tactics that were almost guaranteed to win an acquittal. She didn't know how to defend a client any other way, which was one reason she'd always been very, very careful about whom she chose to represent. Her firm had allowed her that latitude because she'd racked up courtroom victories and a lot of press in the process.

But even as she'd planned Tiny's defense, she'd suffered pangs of guilt. She'd been assailed by doubts. That's why she'd run to Rose Cottage before the trial had begun. It had been eating at her even then. Not that she'd wanted to say it aloud or even allow the thought to form. She'd wanted to go right on believing in Tiny, because she had to in order to live with herself. In retrospect, she knew she should have quit the case the moment she'd had that first niggling doubt, but somehow winning had become more important than anything else, and she'd known she could win.

Now that the truth was out, she was sick of the law, sick of her own ability to twist it for her client's benefit. Her self-respect was in tatters. How had her life come to this? This victory tarnished all the others, all the cases she'd been proud to win, all the cases that had earned her a full partnership at her law firm in record time.

Heartsick, she'd been locked away in her apartment for nearly twenty-four hours now, refusing to answer the phone, refusing to go to the door. She'd given a brief press conference, declaring that she was stunned after the debacle in the courtroom, then gone into hibernation to avoid the inevitable media frenzy over that disturbing courtroom spectacle.

Right now she couldn't imagine ever showing her face again, but realistically she knew that the desire to hide would eventually pass. She was a fighter by nature. She just wasn't ready for battle quite yet. She needed time to lick her wounds in private.

Unfortunately her sisters all had keys to her place, and not five minutes ago they'd arrived en masse to offer her comfort and support. Ashley appreciated the gesture, but it was wasted. She'd gotten a murderer off scot-free, and she was going to have to live with that for the rest of her life. It pretty much made a shambles out of the pride she'd always taken in her success.

"It's not your fault," her sister Jo said quietly, once they were all seated with coffee that Maggie had brewed from the gourmet beans she'd taught them all to appreciate. "You were doing your job."

"A helluva job, isn't it?" Ashley said grimly, lifting her coffee cup in a mocking toast.

"Stop it," Maggie ordered irritably.

Maggie and Melanie had driven up from Virginia the minute they'd heard what happened in the courtroom the day before. They'd picked up Jo on their way into downtown Boston. Ashley had little doubt that they'd planned this gathering down to the last detail on the ride over.

They were seated in Ashley's penthouse apartment with its expensive modern art on the walls and its sweeping panorama of the Boston skyline outside. At the moment, none of it meant a thing to Ashley, not even the loyal support of her sisters. Loyalty was a D'Angelo family trait. They would have been here for her, no matter what she'd done.

"Jo's right. You were doing your job," Melanie said emphatically. "Not everyone who says they're innocent is, not everyone who's accused is guilty, and everyone is guaranteed a right to a complete defense and a fair trial."

How often had she said exactly that? Ashley wondered. She had believed it, too, but knowing that she'd been responsible for putting a violent, totally amoral man back on the streets made her sick.

Having been validated by numerous acquittals from juries, Ashley had gotten used to believing she was always right. She'd grown comfortable looking at the law and its loopholes more intently than the crime and its victims. Maybe that was sound law and a solid defense tactic, but she was beginning to question whether it had anything at all to do with justice.

"The man made a complete fool of me," Ashley told her sisters. "How am I ever supposed to trust my own judgment again? How can anyone else? After this, if I said it was sunny, I'd expect people to check for a second opinion. And what client would want me, knowing that every jury is going to regard me with total skepticism from the outset? It's hard enough to fight the evidence in most cases without the added liability of having a controversial lawyer."

"This was one case out of how many?" Maggie asked, regarding her sister worriedly. "Stop beating yourself up. You have an excellent track record, Ashley. The papers describe you as brilliant, relentless, passionate about the law."

"Not today," Ashley retorted, gesturing toward the stack of newspapers on her coffee table. She'd read them all with a sort of morbid fascination, just as she'd watched every newscast. "Today they're asking questions about how many other criminals I've helped to set free. I have to admit, I've been wondering that myself."

Jo regarded her indignantly. She was the quietest of the D'Angelo sisters, the most sensitive, but when she felt strongly about something, she could make herself heard above their nonstop boisterous chatter.

"Do you really think for one minute that you've intentionally set out to free a bunch of criminals?" Jo demanded. "Because if you do, then you're right. You need to get out of law. You need to find some other field where your mistakes in judgment don't matter, where you can't ever be fooled by a clever client."

"I honestly don't know what I'm doing anymore," Ashley replied. Uncertainty was an unfamiliar feeling, and she didn't like it. She'd always been the D'Angelo with a sense of purpose. She was the confident big sister who protected the rest of them. She didn't like being the object of their pity. She didn't like needing them, rather than the other way around.

"A day ago I would have said I was a champion for the truth," she added. "Now I'm wondering if I'm not just a clever lawyer who's easily duped by a little charm and just the right note of righteous indignation." She stared bleakly around the room. "Look at all this fancy stuff I've accumulated because I'm good at my job. When I had to look the victim's son and daughter in the eye today and tell them I was sorry, I felt like a failure and a fraud."

Her three sisters exchanged a look, then seemed to reach some sort of silent, mutual decision.

"Okay, that's enough self-pity, Ashley. Sackcloth and ashes don't suit you. You're coming back to Virginia with us," Melanie said decisively. "A month or two at Rose Cottage is what you need. You promised Maggie you'd come back after the trial anyway. Now it'll just be for a little longer, until you get your feet back under you."

Ashley stared at her younger sister, horrified by the prospect of an entire week—much less a couple of months—away from work. Work defined her. Of course, today that definition pretty much reeked.

"No way," she said fiercely. "I know you and Maggie thrived while staying in grandmother's old cottage, but I'm not cut out for the boonies. A weekend is about as much as I can take." She scowled at Maggie. "I thought I'd made that clear."

"Hey, you're the one who's been carrying the key around with you as a talisman all these years," Maggie reminded her. "Now it's time you made use of it. Melanie's right—you need to get away. You need to think. You can try to figure out what went wrong this time and stop it from ever happening again. Or you can decide to chuck law and do something else entirely. The one thing we won't let you do is sit around and wallow in self-pity."

"As if there are a lot of other career options open to me," Ashley said bitingly. "I'm a lawyer. That's all I know how to do."

Maggie rolled her eyes. "If you were bright enough to graduate from law school with honors, you can probably find another career in which to excel, if it comes to that. You have to take this break, Ashley. You owe it to yourself. For you to overreact like this, it's obvious you're burned-out. You've been working at a breakneck pace ever since law school in order to jump on that fast track at your law firm. It's time to slow down and reevaluate."

"I agree," Jo said, her jaw set stubbornly. "These two may only be around for a day or two to nudge you, but I'm here for the duration. And I promise I will pester you to death until you agree to take this vacation. In fact, if it were up to me, you'd take a six-month sabbatical."

When Jo, the youngest of them, made such a firm declaration, Ashley knew she was defeated. "Two weeks," she bargained, refusing to even consider as long a leave of absence as Jo was suggesting. "That's all the peace and quiet I can bear."

"Two months," the others chorused.

"Three weeks," she pleaded. "That's it. That's my limit. I'll go nuts if I have to rusticate even one second longer than that."

"Done. Three weeks it is." Maggie and Melanie exchanged a grin.

"What?" Ashley demanded, instantly suspicious of their gloating expressions.

"We were sure you'd bargain us down to a week, max," Maggie said. "You really must be losing your touch."

Ashley started to chuckle, but it came out more like a sob. Wasn't that exactly the point? She *had* lost her touch. And right this minute she couldn't imagine ever getting it back again.

Chapter One

This didn't have to be the worst thing that had ever happened to her, Ashley decided stoically as she stashed groceries into the refrigerator at Rose Cottage.

Two of her sisters and their husbands were close by, so it wouldn't be like she was isolated among strangers. She could always order cable, so she could get Court TV and CNN. She'd brought a case of her favorite wine with her from Boston, along with a year's worth of articles by some of the country's foremost lawyers. She'd even tucked a few novels into her suitcases, books centered around trials, of course.

The key was going to be planning out her days, organizing every minute so she wouldn't have time to think about what had happened in that courtroom back in Boston. Heck, that ought to be a snap. She excelled at organization. That was one reason she'd been able to maintain such a high caseload.

Dispersing those cases among the other partners for the duration of her absence had taken an entire week. She'd worked compulsively to make sure each attorney fully understood her clients' needs. She'd briefed them so thoroughly, they'd seemed a little eager to see her gone.

After that frenetic pace, after loading up the car with all the essentials she couldn't possibly live without and after the long drive, she was just starting to feel a bit of a letdown, that was all. It was to be expected. By morning she'd probably be climbing the walls...or calling the office every five minutes to make sure all the cases she'd left behind were being handled properly. She knew it wouldn't take more than a day for that to wear thin with the already exasperated lawyers she'd left in charge. She would simply have to resist the temptation.

She put her laptop on the kitchen table and placed a stack of legal pads and pens right next to it. It had taken every ounce of willpower she possessed to leave behind her law books, but there was a lot of information to be found on the Internet. She'd make a few notes on her pending cases and pass them along when the time was right.

The mere sight of those familiar tools made her feel better, as if her life hadn't spun wildly out of control.

No sooner was everything in place, though, than Maggie and Melanie swept in the back door, took one look at her stash of supplies and loaded the lot into a shopping bag. They ignored every one of Ashley's heated objections.

"What the hell do the two of you think you're

doing?" she demanded, trying to snatch things back as fast as they picked them up. "This is *my* house. Those are *my* things."

"Actually it's grandmother's house," Maggie reminded her.

"Don't you dare start nitpicking with me," Ashley commanded. "I will leave here."

"No, you won't," Melanie soothed. "You know this is the best possible place for you to be right now."

"And all your precious stuff will be at my place for safekeeping," Maggie promised. "You can have everything back when you leave."

"I need it now if you expect me to stay sane," Ashley protested.

"Forget it," Maggie responded. "And while we're at it, hand over your cell phone."

Ashley felt an unfamiliar hint of panic crawling up her throat. "Come on, Maggie," she pleaded. "I want that stuff. And I've got to have a cell phone. What if somebody needs to reach me?"

Maggie gave her a wry look. "Can you honestly say there's anyone back home besides Mom and Dad and Jo that you're anxious to talk to right now? As for the rest of this, you only need it when you're working."

"And you're on vacation," Melanie reminded her, even as she checked out the stack of reading material Ashley had piled up on the counter. "Sorry. This needs to go, too." She rummaged in Ashley's purse and plucked out the cell phone.

Ashley frowned at the pair of them. "What the hell am I supposed to do for three whole weeks?"

Melanie chuckled. "You're supposed to relax. I

know it's a foreign concept, but you'll get the hang of it eventually."

"I can't sit here all day doing nothing," Ashley protested. "I'll go out of my freaking mind."

"We thought of that," Maggie soothed, handing over a bag filled with videos and paperback novels. "Comedy and romance."

Fluff, nothing but fluff. Ashley moaned. "Dear God, what are you trying to do to me?"

"We're trying to get some balance in your life," Melanie said. "Of course, there's a lot to be done in the garden now. The tulip and daffodil bulbs need to be thinned, and I bought some new ones to be planted out front."

"It's fall, not spring," she reminded Melanie. "Aren't you supposed to plant things in the spring?"

"Not bulbs. They come up early, remember? Trust me, this will be good for you. A little physical work in the sun will take your mind off your problems."

"I don't do physical work," Ashley retorted, glancing at her perfectly manicured nails and trying to imagine them after gardening. She shuddered at the image.

"You go to a gym," Maggie reminded her. "In fact, you're as compulsive about that as you are about everything else. This will be even better for you. You can go for long walks. You'll be breathing in all this fresh, salty air."

"It smells like fish," Ashley retorted, determined not to take pleasure in anything just to spite her hateful sisters. How had she gone all these years without noticing how controlling and obnoxious they were?

Clearly undaunted, Melanie bit back a grin. "Not so much in the garden. You'll see. There are lots of wonderful fragrances out there. Grandmother saw to that and Mike and I recreated it just the way it was."

Defeated, Ashley sat down at the kitchen table and rested her head on her arms. "I want to go home."

"Don't whine," Maggie chided. "It's unbecoming."

Ashley's head snapped up. "You sound exactly like Mom."

"Of course, I do," Maggie said. "We all do, with a touch of Grandmother Lindsey thrown in. They were our role models. The only thing missing is the Southern accent."

Ashley thought back to the subtle lessons their grandmother had instilled in all of them on their visits to Rose Cottage. Cornelia Lindsey had been very big on manners. And, despite the fact that the D'Angelo sisters were growing up in Yankee territory, she'd wanted them to become southern ladies. She'd taught them the importance of family and friendships, of generosity and kindness. Some of the lessons had stuck better than others.

Ashley relented. "Okay, no more whining," she promised. "But you have to get me out of here before I go stir-crazy."

"You just got here two hours ago," Melanie reminded her, looking perplexed.

"And your point is?" Ashley retorted. "In my life, that's a freaking eternity."

"Okay, okay, we'll go to lunch," Maggie soothed. "No wine with lunch, though."

Ashley stared at her. "Why the hell not?"

"Because you don't need it," Melanie said. "You'll want a clear head for all that introspection you intend to do."

"I need the wine for that." Even as she uttered the words, Ashley heard the hint of desperation in her voice and knew it was a warning. She sighed heavily. "Okay, no wine."

Once they were out of the house, Melanie and Maggie refused to let her wallow in self-pity. By the time they'd eaten a leisurely lunch and shopped for a couple of hours, Ashley had actually managed to laugh without restraint a couple times. She'd almost forgotten that this was the first of what promised to be way too many unstructured, unfulfilling days. When she remembered that, she shuddered.

Back at Rose Cottage, Maggie gave her a fierce hug. "You're going to be fine."

"I suppose," Ashley conceded grudgingly. She didn't believe that, not for a minute.

"And we're expecting you for dinner tonight at seven," Maggie added. "I'm making all your favorites. All those dishes Mom used to make for you before you started subsisting on salads." She winked. "Play your cards right, and you can even have a glass of wine."

Ashley laughed. "Now you've made it worth my while to come over and put up with more of these invigorating, if somewhat annoying, pep talks."

Melanie patted her cheek. "Sweetie, we just want you to get yourself back on track. We promise we won't hover, but we will be around if you need us."

"I know and I'm grateful. I really am, even if I have been sounding like a total jerk." She watched them go, taking her laptop, all those articles and her legal pads. She felt a mixture of relief and fear as they disappeared from sight.

Inside, she glanced at the kitchen clock. It was only

two. What on earth was she going to do for five whole hours? What had she done on all those lazy summer afternoons years ago? It finally came to her that when she and her sisters hadn't been out on the water, she'd gone into the backyard with a book in her hand. She'd gotten lost in amazing adventures in exotic locales.

Impulsively she reached into the bag that her sisters had left and withdrew a paperback without even glancing at the title or the author. Neither really mattered.

Before she could suffer a pang of regret or pick up the phone to call the cable company, she went outside to the swing facing the bay. It was wide enough for her to turn sideways and put her feet on the seat, and there was enough breeze to keep it in motion; just a slight, soothing back and forth.

She opened the book, read the first paragraph with the intention of hating it, then read the second with a more open mind. By the end of the page, she was hooked. She was reminded of the pleasure she'd felt years ago when her days had been lazy and undemanding and a good story had been all she needed to keep herself entertained for hours on end.

The best days had been the rainy ones, when she'd curled up on a chair in the living room or on the porch, book in hand, a glass of freshly squeezed lemonade beside her. She'd read incessantly, emerging only long enough for meals or to play cards or board games with her grandmother and sisters.

The satisfaction of that was coming back to her, page by page. In this book, the characters jumped off the page, the romance was steamy and the author's voice was filled with intelligence and wit. Ashley lost herself in the story.

She was stiff and cramped when she finally turned the last page. Her cheeks were unexpectedly damp with happy tears. When was the last time she'd read anything that had affected her like this? Probably before she'd gone to law school. Since then she hadn't had time for the simple pleasure of reading for entertainment.

For the very first time, Ashley saw this self-imposed banishment in a new light, as a real gift. Maybe if she went back to the girl she'd once been, to someone who was filled with hopes and dreams, she'd be able to discover where she'd slipped off track. Maybe she'd rediscover the humanity that had made her a good judge of people before she'd started to rely on cool calculation and mental agility to succeed.

Not that she intended to tell her sisters that she was beginning to see the benefits of this sabbatical. They'd gloat.

"Oh, my gosh, dinner," she muttered, glancing at her watch. It was ten minutes till seven, and she'd never even taken a shower or changed. After all her grumbling about the mere thought of being isolated, if she was late for a party, she'd never hear the end of it.

"They'll just have to take me as I am," she said, laughing at the evidence that she was already adopting a whole new attitude.

That didn't stop Ashley from grabbing her purse and car keys and tearing out of the driveway at her more accustomed frantic pace. She simply couldn't be expected to change everything about her personality overnight.

Josh felt like a rebellious twelve-year-old running away from home and unwanted responsibilities. As he neared the Chesapeake Bay, he could smell the tang of salt water in the cool September air. As he got closer to his family's longtime second home by the water, there was also a faintly fishy scent that he'd come to acquaint with summer. His mother had balanced that with a garden filled with fragrant blossoms, which were just beginning to fade as summer moved into autumn.

When he turned at last onto the final leg of the journey, a long, winding country road that led from White Stone toward Windmill Point, he spotted a dozen or so brand-new homes interspersed with the old cottages and other recently completed vacation homes. The new additions were huge, dwarfing their quaint and occasionally run-down neighbors, but large or small, they all shared the same incredible view of the Chesapeake Bay and its inlets.

He was almost to the cutoff to Idylwild, the small clapboard cottage with its neat green shutters and sweeping porch, when a fancy car being driven toward him way too fast took the turn ahead of him wide. The driver spotted him too late and tried to overcorrect. Josh cut the wheel in the opposite direction, but the crunch of metal against metal was inevitable, the contact jarring but not enough to cause injury.

He leapt out of the car in full lawyer mode, then backed up a step at the sight of the tawny-haired driver of the other car suddenly bursting into tears. At once all he could think about were broken bones and soft, bleeding skin.

"Are you okay?" he asked, leaning in the driver's window close enough to catch a faint whiff of something exotic, sexy and expensive. The combination dealt a knockout punch to his belly and put the rest of his all-too-male senses on full alert.

Brown eyes, shimmering with tears, glanced up at him, then away. Her cheeks blazed with unmistakable embarrassment. Josh studied her, trying to figure out why he felt an almost immediate connection to her, as if they'd known each other before. But that couldn't be, of course. He would have remembered any woman who looked like this. Except for the tear-streaked face, she was as sleek and polished as any of the society women he'd come to know in Richmond. The clothes were expensive, if wrinkled. Gold-and-diamond studs winked from her ears.

"I'm so sorry," she whispered. "It was my fault." She was already fumbling in her Gucci bag, apparently digging for her driver's license, car registration and insurance card. "Dammit, dammit, dammit! Why can't I ever find anything in here?"

"It's okay," Josh soothed, sensing that she was about to burst into another noisy round of sobs that would claw at his gut. "There's no rush. We're in the country. Folks around here don't get all worked up over a little fender bender. We can take care of the formalities in a minute. How about some bottled water? I just picked up a case of the stuff. It's warm, but it might help. I have a first-aid kit, too. We can take care of that scrape on your cheek."

She self-consciously touched her hand to her face, then stared at the blood with shock. She immediately turned pale.

"Hold on," Josh said. "Don't you dare faint on me. It's nothing. Just a tiny little cut." He glanced inside the car, trying to figure out if anything was broken. He couldn't see any glass that would explain the injury.

Without waiting for a reply, he ran back to his ridiculously oversize but trendy SUV, retrieved a bottle of water, some peroxide and antibiotic cream, then went back. By then, the other driver had emerged from behind the wheel, all five-ten or so of her, with narrow hips and endless legs and just enough curves to make a man's blood stir with interest.

"I'm Josh," he said when he could get his tongue untangled. He handed her the water. He poured the peroxide on a cotton ball and reached over to touch the wound, but she immediately tried to take the cotton from him.

"I'll do it," she said.

"You can't see what you're doing," he said, holding firm and cupping her chin in his other hand, then daubing the peroxide on the scrape. He bit back a grin when she winced even before he'd made contact.

"There, that wasn't so bad, was it?" he asked when he'd cleaned the wound.

She frowned at him.

"You never did say what your name is," he reminded her as he smoothed on antibiotic cream, trying not to linger on her soft-as-silk skin.

"Ashley."

He heard the unmistakable Boston accent. "Just visiting the area?"

"For three weeks," she said emphatically, as if that were two-and-a-half weeks too long. "Are you a local?"

"I like to think of myself as one," he said. Richmond might be where he lived, but this was the home of his heart. He hadn't realized how much he'd missed it until he'd made that final turn onto this road leading to the cottage where he'd spent some of the happiest summers of his life. He'd finally felt as if all the problems that had sent him scurrying down here were falling into perspective.

"Either you are or you aren't," she said, studying him with a narrowed gaze.

Amused by her need for precision, Josh said, "I've pretty much grown up around here."

"Then you probably know the sheriff or whoever we need to call to report this," she said.

"Let's take a look and see if it's even worth reporting," he suggested. He examined first her car and then his own, concluding that they were both in need of new front bumpers and maybe a paint touch-up, but that both cars had escaped serious damage.

"Look, why don't we call this even?" he suggested.

"Because I caused it," she said, grimly determined to take responsibility. "I should deal with all the damages."

"That's why we carry insurance," he corrected. "You deal with your company. I'll deal with mine. It might not even be worth it, though. A body shop could fix things up for next to nothing."

"But I should pay whatever it costs," she insisted.

Josh couldn't seem to stop himself from suggesting, "Then have dinner with me one night while you're here. We'll pick someplace outrageously expensive, and you can buy if it'll make you feel better."

She murmured something under her breath, but finally nodded..

Josh studied her curiously. "What did you say?"

"I said you're obviously not a lawyer, or you'd be all over this, milking it for every dime you could get in damages."

He laughed. "That's just about the nicest compliment anyone's paid me in months," he said, deciding then and there that not being a lawyer for a bit suited him just fine. It wasn't that far from the truth. Wasn't that precisely why he'd come here, to figure out if he wanted to be a lawyer anymore with all that it entailed, including his expected engagement to his boss's daughter?

"Do you have a phone number, Ashley? I'll call you about dinner."

She jotted it down, but before she handed it to him, she added something else, "If you change your mind about my paying for the damage to your car, I won't fight you."

Josh glanced at the paper and saw that she'd written, "My fault. I owe you," then signed her name in the kind of illegible scrawl usually used by physicians.

"A confession?" he asked, amused. "Think it would hold up in court?"

"It would if I wanted it to," she said flatly, then lowered herself gracefully into her car, giving him one last intoxicating view of those incredibly long legs. "See you around."

"Oh, you can count on that," Josh said, fingering the piece of paper she'd given him.

He stood watching until she was out of sight, then tucked the piece of paper into his pocket and gave it a pat. Coming home was turning out to be one of the smartest decisions he'd made in a long time.

And ironically the past couple of minutes had already given him insight into one of those important decisions he was here to consider. If he could feel this powerful tug of attraction to a woman who'd just creamed his beloved car, then the very last thing he ought to be considering was marriage to Stephanie Lockport Williams. First thing in the morning, he'd have to call and make it clear to her that despite her father's wishes, they had no future.

And right after that, he'd call the mysterious Ashley and invite her out for a crab feast. There was no better way to get to know a woman than watching her handle the messy task of picking crabs. Stephanie had flatly refused to touch the things, which should have told Josh all he needed to know months ago.

Something told him that Ashley would show no such restraint. In fact, he had a hunch she'd go after those crabs with all the passion and enthusiasm of a local. There was something wildly seductive in watching a woman hammer away at the hard shells, then delicately pick out the sweet meat and dip it in melted butter, then savor every bite. He thought of Ashley's lush lips closing around a chunk of backfin crabmeat dripping in butter, and concluded it was definitely a spectacle he could hardly wait to see.

Chapter Two

"Stupid, stupid, stupid," Ashley muttered as she sat with Maggie on the porch of the farmhouse Maggie and Rick lived in a few miles from Rose Cottage. It had an orchard out back, the trees laden down with ripe apples. The sun was beginning to drop in the western sky, splashing everything with orange light. It was so serene, it should have creeped Ashley out, but she had other things on her mind, like that ridiculous accident she'd caused by driving too fast on an unfamiliar winding road. For a split second she'd lost her concentration, and that had been enough to nearly cause a tragedy. There would have been no adequate defense for it.

"What is *wrong* with me?" she asked her sister plaintively.

Maggie glanced at her husband. Both of them were fighting a grin.

"What?" Ashley demanded. "Why are you two laughing at me?"

"We're not laughing at you," Maggie rushed to assure her. "It's just that the saint is discovering she's human. It's a wonderful thing to see. I, for one, never thought it would happen. I can't wait to tell Melanie and Mike when they get here."

Ashley gave her sister a sour look. "You know, if you keep this up, you're going to make me sorry I agreed to come to Virginia for five minutes, much less three weeks," she told Maggie irritably. "I can go back to Boston first thing in the morning, you know."

"But you won't," Maggie said.

Ashley found her confidence annoying. "Oh? Why is that, Ms. Know-it-all?"

"You made a deal with us. If you break it, then we'll know you're in some sort of emotional meltdown that probably requires hospitalization."

Ashley scowled. "Not even remotely funny."

"I didn't mean it to be," Maggie assured her. "You need this sabbatical, Ashley, and one way or another we're going to see to it that you take it. Rose Cottage is much cheaper and a whole lot more pleasant than some quiet sanitarium in a tranquil setting with shrinks watching your every move." She let that image sink in, then asked, "Don't you agree?"

Ashley stared hard at her sister to see if she was joking. She didn't appear to be. "You wouldn't do that to me."

"If it was the only way to assure that you get some

rest, we would," Maggie retorted emphatically. "Don't test us. That's how worried we are about you."

"Mom and Dad would never allow it," Ashley said.

"Are you so sure of that? They're worried sick, too."

"I'm not having a damn breakdown, though you could easily drive me to one," Ashley said, barely keeping a grip on her temper. The last thing she needed to do was give them ammunition to have her committed. And they *would* do it. She could see that now. There was no mistaking the resolve in Maggie's eyes.

"You're not having one *yet*," Maggie agreed. "But you're on the verge, Ashley. None of us have ever seen you strung this tight before. Everyone has their limits. What happened in court was only the final blow. You've been pushing yourself too hard for too long."

"I think we need to change the subject before you really get on my nerves," Ashley told her sister. She deliberately turned to Rick. "Do you know of a Josh around here?"

Rick looked as if he didn't really want to be drawn into the conversation, even if the subject seemed to be neutral. Ashley could hardly blame him. When he shrugged, she turned back to Maggie. "What about you? Do you know a Josh?"

"Is that the man you hit?" Maggie asked.

Ashley nodded.

"No last name?"

"He didn't offer one," Ashley said, then remembered the exchange of notes. Maybe he had written it down. "Wait. Here it is. Madison. Josh Madison."

Maggie's expression turned thoughtful. "There were some Madisons who had a summer place not far from

Rose Cottage. I think Grandma knew them. Maybe he's related to them. That would certainly explain why he was on that road. Melanie and Mike might know him."

"I suppose that's possible," Ashley said. "But he said he was local."

"Maybe he is now," Rick finally chimed in. "But I don't recall the name, and I talk to a lot of people around the area. I could ask Willa-Dean next time I go to Callao for lunch. That girl knows everybody, especially the single men."

Ashley shook her head. "No need. I doubt we'll even cross paths again, unless he changes his mind about me paying for the damage to his car."

Maggie grinned. "Why so interested, Ash? Is he gorgeous? Sexy?"

"Nice," Ashley said, refusing to be drawn into a discussion of Josh Madison's appeal. *Nice* was safe. *Nice* didn't stir up hormones.

Unfortunately, Josh Madison was a bit more than nice. As rattled as she'd been by that stupid accident, she'd noted that he was sexy and gorgeous, just as her sister had guessed. Not that Ashley cared, of course. Men were the last thing on her mind these days. But accepting that didn't mean she couldn't appreciate a fine specimen when one happened to cross her path, even if this one was clearly not her type.

After all, he'd been dressed in a faded T-shirt and equally faded jeans, with boat shoes and no socks. It wasn't a look that appealed to her. She was drawn to men in designer suits and expensive imported footwear. She was drawn to men who reeked of ambition and success. Josh Madison looked…normal. Just an everyday guy. Ashley didn't do ordinary.

Not that she'd done all that well with the overly ambitious type, either. The one serious relationship in her life had been with a man every bit as driven to succeed as she was. He'd worn all the right clothes, gone to all the right places, been seen with all the right people.

But Drew Wellington turned out to have this nasty habit of lying to her, hiding things from her such as the supposedly unimportant detail that he had a high-school sweetheart back home whom he saw every chance he got. He'd also failed to mention that his old flame was pregnant with his child.

Not that he intended to marry her. She wasn't suitable, he'd tried to explain to Ashley when she'd discovered his tawdry little secret. Ashley was the woman he wanted to marry.

She wasn't sure which part of that had made her sickest, the lying or the snobbery, but the betrayal had all come flooding back to her in that courtroom a week ago when she'd realized that her ex and Tiny shared a common lack of familiarity with the truth. What was it about her that made people think they didn't have to be honest with her? Did they think she was too stupid to discover the lies, or that she wouldn't care if she did?

Either way, she definitely hadn't done so well with her one foray into love of the proper kind. Still, that didn't mean she was ready to start compromising her ideals for a man utterly lacking in style and ambition, even if that did make her into the very kind of snob she claimed to despise.

Which was unfortunate, she concluded when Melanie and Mike arrived not five minutes later with Josh Madison in tow. Her heart promptly began the kind of enthusiastic staccato rhythm she hadn't felt in years. Josh had cleaned up nicely. His hair was damp and spiked with gel, his cheeks were smooth and he'd changed into chinos and an expensive knit shirt with a designer logo emblazoned discreetly on the pocket. He was still wearing the disreputable-looking boat shoes, though, and no socks.

"Look who we found," Melanie announced cheerfully. "We ran into Josh on our way over and invited him to tag along. He's our neighbor. You guys must remember the Madison house. And Josh remembers Grandma Lindsey. Hope you don't mind, Maggie, but we didn't want to leave him on his own. I know you always cook enough for a mob."

Ashley frowned at Maggie, who was struggling unsuccessfully to contain a chuckle.

"I think it's great," Maggie enthused. "I just hope you didn't run into Josh the same way Ashley did earlier. I doubt his car could take another encounter like that."

Melanie's eyes widened as she turned from Josh to Ashley and back again. "Ashley is the person who hit you?"

Ashley turned her scowl on Josh. "Couldn't wait to spread the word, I see."

"Actually, I didn't volunteer anything. Mike noticed the dent and asked about it," he said. "Would you have wanted me to lie to him?"

She sighed at that. "Of course not."

He regarded her speculatively. "I hope it's not going to make you uncomfortable having to sit across a dinner table from me?"

Ashley frowned. He seemed to be relishing the

prospect of causing her a little discomfort. "Absolutely not," she lied.

Josh grinned. "You can always think of it as that penance you were so anxious to exact from yourself earlier," he suggested. "Though don't think tonight will get you off the hook on that *other* dinner you promised me. I'm counting on that."

Maggie and Melanie stared at them, clearly fascinated by the exchange. They were going to make way too much of this, Ashley could tell. She needed to defuse their speculation as quickly as possible.

"Whatever," she said with a very deliberate shrug of indifference. "I can stand it if you can. I'm used to uncomfortable situations."

"She's used to staring down prosecutors," Melanie explained. "She's very good at it."

Josh's grin spread. "A lawyer. I should have guessed. It explains a lot."

Normally she would have challenged him on a remark like that, but Ashley was in no mood to be drawn into the kind of passionate debate that might be misinterpreted by her sisters as some sort of chemistry. Instead, she reminded them mildly, "But right now, as I have been repeatedly told, I'm on vacation." She turned her gaze on Maggie. "By the way, I'm starved. Didn't you say something about dinner when you invited us over here, Maggie? Or was that some bait-and-switch thing?"

"See, there you are in lawyer mode again," Maggie retorted. "How are we supposed to forget if you can't?"

Ashley could see her point. "I'm working on it," she swore. "I really am." But something told her it was going to be easier said than done.

When she glanced at Josh, she caught a commiserating look in his eyes. It seemed as if he actually understood what she was going through, and that made her wonder if she'd totally misjudged him. Then again, maybe that kind of sensitivity merely went along with being nice. Neither were traits with which she had a lot of experience. Drew had been smart and savvy and sophisticated, but definitely not nice. Her male colleagues were brilliant and clever but rarely nice, and hardly ever sensitive or considerate.

"Something tells me there's a story behind that," Josh said quietly, his expression thoughtful.

"Not one we're going to get into tonight," Maggie said decisively. She turned to Ashley. "Since you're so anxious to eat, Ashley, you can help me in the kitchen. Rick, get Josh a glass of wine."

Ashley reluctantly followed her sister into the kitchen. She knew precisely what was coming, especially since Melanie was right on her heels.

"First day in town and you find yourself a keeper," Maggie taunted as she handed Ashley another place setting.

"Don't be ridiculous," Ashley retorted. "We don't know anything about him."

Melanie beamed. "That's why it's so nice that you have all this time on your hands to change that."

"Even if I were interested—and I am definitely not saying that I am—what makes you think Josh doesn't already have a girlfriend?"

"Oh, please," Maggie said. "Have you seen the way the man looks at you? It's as if he can't quite believe his luck."

"Drew used to look at me like that, too," Ashley commented wryly.

"No, he didn't," Maggie responded, her voice laced with derision. "Drew looked at you as if you were a particularly valuable possession he'd acquired along with his BMW and his Rolex."

Ashley couldn't deny Maggie's take on the past, but she rolled her eyes anyway. "Could we just get through dinner with the least amount of humiliation possible? Do not try to foist me off on Josh like some pathetic thing who needs to be entertained."

"I won't have to," Maggie said confidently. "You'll see. Josh strikes me as the kind of man who'll take things into his own hands if he gets the slightest bit of encouragement from you. Hasn't he already gotten you to agree to have dinner with him?"

"Yes, but—"

"I rest my case," Maggie said, her triumph plain.

"I am not here to encourage some man I've barely met," Ashley insisted.

"I agree with Maggie. Just open yourself up to the possibilities," Melanie pleaded. "That's all we're asking. Now go set a place for Josh, then sit down right next to it. Maggie and I will get dinner on the table."

Ashley laughed despite herself. "You two never give up, do you? Just because you landed fantastic men doesn't mean everyone has to settle down to be happy. It's possible to be single and totally fulfilled."

"Maybe," Maggie conceded with obvious skepticism, "but you can't blame us for wanting you to be as happy as we are. You nudged me and Rick together. Now it's my chance to return the favor. Melanie's, too."

"I don't consider this a favor," Ashley said, giving it one last try.

Maggie smiled serenely. "Something tells me you will," she said.

Melanie nodded in agreement, then added with a grin, "Eventually, anyway."

Josh noted that Ashley had managed to seat herself at the opposite end of the table from him, much to her sister Maggie's very evident dismay. He, on the other hand, was a little relieved. The woman overwhelmed him. He literally needed some space between them so he could catch his breath.

Besides, he hadn't made that call to Stephanie yet. It was a point of honor with him that he needed to officially break things off with her before he moved on. If Ashley were too close, he might toss aside his better judgment and try to figure out some way to crawl directly into her bed before the night was over. That kind of reckless, breakneck pace was a very bad thing, especially for a man who had supposedly taken some vacation time to make some tough decisions about his future.

He'd always been a plodder, taking things slowly, thinking them through. He'd just about thought the whole engagement thing to death, which was one reason—thankfully—that it had never happened.

The woman sitting opposite him made him want to seize the moment, which was a very scary proposition. When he'd agreed to come to dinner tonight, he'd had no idea that Ashley would be here. The hop, skip and jump of his pulse when he'd spotted her dented car in the driveway had been way too telling. He was about to throw caution to the wind. The length of the dinner table and the presence of four obviously fascinated observers were the only things standing in his way.

Well, those things and that look of distress in Ashley's amazing eyes, which had turned a golden topaz in the candlelight. She was clearly vulnerable and hurting. It evidently had something to do with her career. Since his own was likely to go up in flames as soon as he broke things off with Stephanie, he could relate to Ashley's professional uncertainty.

Brevard, Williams and Davenport was one of Richmond's premier law firms. Josh had been proud when they'd hired him straight out of law school, then promoted him quickly. But it had been increasingly evident that his future there was directly tied in to his relationship with Stephanie. If he broke up with her this weekend, he was very likely to be fired on Monday. The thought didn't terrify him nearly as much as he'd expected it to. In fact, when he could ignore the churning in his gut, it seemed to give him an amazing sense of freedom.

"You're awfully quiet," Mike said. "You sure you didn't bump your head in that accident?"

Josh shrugged off his concern. "Just thinking about how life takes a lot of unexpected twists."

Mike glanced over at Melanie, and his entire expression softened. "Indeed, it does."

"How long have the two of you been married?" Josh asked him.

"Four months."

"Long engagement?"

Mike grinned. "Hardly. We just met in March."

Josh stared at him in shock. "You seem like you've known each other forever."

"I guess that's the way it is when you meet the right woman," Mike said. "What do you think, Rick?"

Rick blinked and dragged his gaze away from his wife. "What?"

Mike chuckled. "Josh and I were discussing whirlwind courtships."

Rick laughed. "You're definitely asking the experts. Maggie and I were together for, what, a couple of months?"

Josh's jaw dropped. "And you've been married how long?"

"About four weeks," Rick said. "The D'Angelo women don't waste a lot of time. A smart man seizes the moment when they're around."

Josh fell silent, staring at the three women at the opposite end of the table, their heads together. How had he missed it? Of course, the three women were more than just friends. They were sisters. Melanie had even said as much when she'd referred to their grandmother Lindsey earlier. He'd been fooled by the different last names or maybe by the fact that they'd all grown up into such vibrant but distinctive women.

As girls, they'd been cookie-cutter versions of each other, varying only in height. Oh, they'd been gorgeous enough to catch his attention and leave him tongue-tied, but they'd worn their hair in similar styles and dressed in variations of the same shorts and halter tops. Back then, there had been no mistaking the family resemblance. In fact, only those who knew them well could keep them straight. Josh hadn't known them at all. They'd been on the periphery of his life, a taunting reminder of what an outsider he was.

Josh studied them quizzically, then asked Mike, "Isn't there another sister?"

"Jo," he said at once. "She still lives in Boston. You knew the D'Angelo sisters, growing up?" Mike asked.

"Not really. It's more like I knew of them. We didn't exactly travel in the same circles."

"But didn't Melanie say your family knew their grandmother?" Rick asked.

"Fairly well, as a matter of fact," Josh admitted. "But you know how kids are. They find their own friends, especially in the summertime around here." Determined to move on, he asked, "How did you meet them?"

"Maggie and I met in Boston," Rick said. "I stepped in at the last minute to handle a photo shoot for her magazine. She came down here, and I followed her."

"Melanie and I met here," Mike explained. "She was staying at Rose Cottage for a bit." He grinned. "Sort of the way Ashley's staying there now for a little R and R."

Rick gave Josh a considering look, then added pointedly, "History tends to repeat itself at Rose Cottage."

Not this time, Josh thought. Not that he wasn't attracted to Ashley. He was. Not that he didn't intend to see more of her while she was here. He did.

But his life was in chaos, and something told him hers was, as well. That made it a very bad time to be thinking in other than the most immediate terms. Dinner. A few laughs. That kind of thing.

When he glanced around the table, he noticed that four pairs of eyes were regarding him way too speculatively. The only eyes that counted, however, were watching him with unmistakable wariness. Clearly, Ashley was no more inclined to be railroaded into a relationship than he was. And wasn't that all that mattered?

"Maybe you and Ashley should get together to work out a settlement for the damages from the accident," Maggie suggested without any attempt at subtlety.

"We've taken care of that," Ashley replied at once.

To his shock and dismay, a streak of totally unfamiliar perversity sliced through Josh. "I've been thinking maybe we were a little too hasty. Neither of us was thinking too clearly."

"I was thinking just fine," Ashley retorted. "I offered to pay for all the damages since it was my fault. That offer still stands."

"As a lawyer, you should know an offer like that could open you up to exorbitant demands," Josh countered. "You've admitted guilt. You couldn't possibly have been thinking clearly or you would never have done such a thing."

"I was taking responsibility for my actions," she retorted. "You turned me down." Her gaze narrowed. "Are you changing your mind? Suddenly feeling the onset of whiplash, perhaps?" she inquired tartly.

If it would keep the fire in her eyes, Josh would have prolonged the argument as long as possible, but they were being watched with total fascination by everyone else at the table. He didn't want to encourage the meddlers.

"Possibly," he equivocated, rubbing his neck. Sure enough, sparks of indignation lit her eyes.

"Well, be sure to let me know when you've made up your mind," Ashley replied, a hint of sarcasm in her tone. "Why is it that men can never make a decision about anything?"

"Hey," Rick and Mike protested in unison. "Don't turn this into some sort of gender war and drag the rest of us into it," Mike went on.

"Uh-oh," Maggie said. "Watch your step, Ashley. You're about to unite these men in a common cause. Something tells me it won't be pretty."

"Doggone right," Josh agreed, suddenly eager to stir the pot. "Men are not the problem. We think logically and rationally."

"Oh, please," Ashley said. "What was logical or rational about letting me off the hook so easily?"

"You were clearly shaken up. I was trying to be a nice guy," Josh retorted.

"Ha!" Ashley muttered.

"Women hate that," Rick advised.

"They see it as a sign of weakness," Mike confirmed.

"Well, you can be sure I won't make that mistake again," Josh vowed. "I thought you were a reasonable woman."

"I am. You're the one behaving like an idiot. You're no more injured than I am."

He frowned at her. "You're calling me an idiot?"

"You bet I am."

As the exchange ended and her declaration hung in the air, Ashley suddenly blinked and looked embarrassed. "What just happened here?"

Maggie grinned at them. "Offhand, I'd say we just witnessed an explosion of hormones. I, for one, found it rather fascinating."

"Stimulating," Melanie added, casting a pointed look at her husband.

Before Josh could utter a desperate denial, Ashley

whirled on her sisters. "Eat dirt," she muttered, then stood up. "I have to go."

Josh was way too tempted to follow her. Instead, he merely winked as she passed. "Drive safely," he murmured under his breath.

She stopped and scowled at him. He waited for her to utter the curse that was obviously on the tip of her tongue, but she fought it and won.

"Lovely seeing you again," she said sweetly. Her voice, thick with Southern syrup, nonetheless lacked sincerity.

"I'm sure we'll cross paths soon," Josh said. "Hopefully without colliding."

Though he had to admit, as he watched her walk away, that bumping into Ashley D'Angelo, literally or figuratively, was starting to make his life a whole lot livelier.

Chapter Three

Fresh from his second disconcerting, intriguing encounter with Ashley D'Angelo, Josh knew he couldn't delay the inevitable talk with Stephanie for another minute. That explosion of hormones Maggie had referred to had been very real. It had been a couple of hours now, and he was still half-aroused when he thought about it. Stephanie had never had that effect on him. They'd been friends who'd understood what was expected of them and accepted that real passion wasn't part of it.

Even as he reached for the phone, he acknowledged that it was probably a conversation he should be having face-to-face. Since he didn't plan on being back in Richmond for a while, though, he wanted to get it over with now, tonight. Something told him that by morning, or at least by the time he had his next encounter with Ashley, he should be totally free from the past.

Fortunately, Stephanie was a night owl. Even though it was after eleven, he knew she'd be awake. What he hadn't expected, though, was the sound of a party in full swing in the background when she answered. She sounded carefree and happy, happier than he could recall her being in a long time. Somehow when they were together, she always seemed subdued and thoughtful.

"Steph, it's me," he said.

"Josh, sweetheart, I wasn't expecting to hear from you this late."

"Evidently." He had no idea why he couldn't seem to keep the edge out of his voice. He wasn't jealous. No, if anything, he was relieved. Maybe this odd mood he was suddenly in simply had to do with the possibility that now wasn't the best time to have this conversation, after all. "Look, you obviously have company. Maybe I should call back in the morning."

"Don't be silly. It's just a few friends kicking back on a Friday night. I'll just go into the other room, where I can hear better."

The music and laughter grew more muffled. "There. That's better," she said. "How's it going? Are you having a good time? Are you getting all that deep thinking done?"

"Some of it," he said.

"I wish you'd let me come with you. Maybe I could have helped. You've always liked bouncing ideas off of me in the past."

"Normally that's true," he said, "but not this time. I had to work this out on my own."

"You're thinking about us, aren't you?" she asked, sounding resigned but not surprised.

Josh had always known that Stephanie was smart and intuitive, but he hadn't expected her to cut right to the chase on this one. "Yes," he admitted. "I think we need to talk about where we're headed."

"Okay," she said.

"I owe you better than a conversation on the phone, but I didn't want to wait till I get back."

"Come on, Josh, just say it and get it over with," she chided.

"I know your father is counting on us announcing our engagement soon and that we've been talking about it for a long time now," he began. "But I think you and I both know that he's more enthusiastic about the idea than either of us are."

His words were greeted with silence.

"Stephanie?"

"What are you saying, Josh?" she asked.

He sucked in a deep breath and forced himself to be brutally honest. "That we're all wrong for each other, Steph. We both know it. We've been trying to make the pieces fit, but they don't. This isn't your fault, Stephanie. You're amazing. It's me. I want something else. I wish I could explain it better than that, but I can't. I only know this isn't fair to either one of us. I need to let you go, and I feel sure you'll be far happier with someone else."

"I see," she said softly.

She didn't sound half as brokenhearted as he'd feared she might. "I'm sorry," he apologized.

"No need to be," she said, sounding oddly relieved.

Josh was astounded that she was taking his announcement so well. He'd expected tears or histrionics. In fact, he'd been dreading a messy emotional scene, if only because he was throwing a monkey wrench into her father's plans for the two of them, and Stephanie was, first and foremost, a dutiful daughter who understood what was expected of her.

"Do you mean that?" he asked, still not quite believing that the breakup could go so smoothly.

"To be honest, I've seen this coming," she confessed. "It's something I should have done myself, but I've never had the courage to defy my father. I guess I owe you for making it easy."

"You're really okay with this?" he asked.

"Were you hoping I'd fight you?" she asked, sounding amused.

"No, of course not, but—"

She laughed. "No buts, darling. You're off the hook. I'm weak, not stupid. To be perfectly honest, I've known for months now that we're not a good match, not for the long term. I guess I was hoping that Daddy was right, because you are so damn nice."

Josh was getting a little tired of being nice tonight. Nice guys usually finished last. Sometimes he wondered if that wasn't why he was so uncomfortable in a courtroom. He hated going for the jugular. He preferred mediation to confrontation.

"You're probably letting me off too easy," he told her. "I doubt your father will be half as understanding. Would you like me to explain all this to him?"

"Forget about Daddy. I'll talk to him," Stephanie assured him. "I won't let him kick you out of the firm over this."

"You don't need to go to bat for me," Josh said. "I'll handle your father if I decide I want to stay on."

"*If?* You're thinking about quitting your job?" she asked, clearly far more shocked by that than by his decision to break up with her.

"Actually I am," he admitted. "But I'm trying not to do anything hasty." He was a plodder, after all. He liked knowing that all his ducks were in a row before doing anything too drastic. It had taken his immediate and intense attraction to Ashley to get him to make this decision. Otherwise he might have drifted along indecisively for a while longer just because being with Stephanie was comfortable.

"I do love you, you know," she told him. "Just not the way you ought to be loved. And I want you to be happy."

"I want the same for you." He recalled the lively sounds of the party. "Something tells me you won't have to wait too long."

"What about you?" she said. "What kind of woman do you really want?"

An image of Ashley resurfaced for about the hundredth time since they'd met that afternoon. He wasn't about to mention it, though. He wasn't that foolish. Stephanie might be taking the breakup with a great deal of grace, but he doubted she'd like knowing that he'd found a replacement already.

"I'll let you know when I've figured that out," he promised.

She laughed. "Please do. Will you call me when you get back to Richmond?"

"Sure, if you want me to."

"I'd like us to stay friends," she told him with unmistakable sincerity. "You're the best one I ever had. I'm not sure I realized that until tonight, when you set me free."

"Then this is a good thing for both of us?" he asked, still worried a bit by her calm demeanor.

"It really is," she assured him. "Now go out there and find the woman who's really right for you, and I'll dance at your wedding."

"You're amazing," he said sincerely.

"I know," she said, laughing. "I think I'm just now figuring that out, too."

Josh hung up and sighed. Relief washed over him. That had gone a thousand times better than he'd anticipated. If only all the other decisions on his plate would go half as smoothly.

Ashley had scrubbed the kitchen floor, cleaned out the refrigerator, rearranged the cupboards and even considered the bags of bulbs that Melanie had surreptitiously left on the back steps. She might be going stir-crazy, but she wasn't quite ready for a close encounter with the garden worms just yet.

Still, it was barely mid-morning, and she'd already done every single thing she could think of to do inside the house. She'd passed her limit on coffee for the morning and eaten a bran muffin and a banana, which was more than she'd usually consumed by this hour.

Normally by late morning, she'd been to the gym and had already been at her desk for hours. There was little question that exercise was what she needed now to take the edge off the stress.

Suddenly she recalled the kayak that used to be stored in what had once been a garage but was too small to accommodate anything other than the smallest of today's vehicles. She found the key to the lock and opened the creaky door. Sure enough, the kayak was still inside, along with its paddle.

Pushing aside all the boxes that had been stored around it, she finally managed to drag the kayak out. She hosed it down, then dragged it to the water's edge. She found a baseball cap on a hook in the kitchen, retrieved the paddle from the old garage, then climbed into the kayak and shoved off, praying that paddling was like riding a bicycle, something one never forgot.

At first she stayed close to shore to be sure the kayak was still seaworthy and hadn't sprung any leaks over the years. When she was finally satisfied that it wasn't going to sink and that she still had the hang of paddling it, she grew more ambitious.

The September sun was beating down on her bare shoulders and glaring off the water. She wiped the sweat off her brow and paused long enough to twist her hair into a knot on top of her head and stuff it under the cap, then began to paddle in earnest.

It took Ashley some time to find her rhythm and longer to move at a pace that provided real exercise. When her arms and shoulders started aching, she let the kayak drift, leaned back and closed her eyes. The sun felt good now that it was being tempered by a breeze. Her body felt energized and, in an odd way, lazy at the same time. Maybe this was what relaxing felt like. If so, she might be able to get used to it eventually.

A part of her immediately rebelled at the thought. She wasn't going to get used to this. She needed excitement and challenges. This was just a little break, a chance to regroup.

To prove her point, she sat up straight, grabbed the paddle and put herself into the task of rowing back to the cottage. She was not about to turn into some goalless, lazy slacker, not even here. Not even for three weeks.

Her sisters might have taken away her legal pads and her pencils, but the stores in town would have more. Suddenly it seemed vital that she get new supplies and put her nose to the grindstone. Pleasant as it was, she was wasting time out here.

Her enthusiasm waned almost as quickly as it had peaked when she realized that she had no real work to do. She was supposed to be thinking, contemplating her future, but the idea held no appeal at all. She could make lists and prioritize all she wanted to, but something told her she would only be floundering right now. Her brain really did need a break.

Well, hell, she thought, letting the paddle fall idle as tears stung her eyes. She brushed at them impatiently and took up the paddle again. Dammit, she was not going to wallow in self-pity. If she couldn't excel at law right now, then she could excel at kayaking, she decided with grim determination. Maybe the world had enough lawyers anyway…at least for a few more weeks.

His situation with Stephanie resolved, Josh had finally let his thoughts turn to Ashley. It had taken him a ridiculously long time the night before to get it straight that all three women in the room were D'Angelos and that they were the granddaughters of Mrs. Lindsey, the woman who'd been a good friend of his own grandmother.

As a kid, he'd envied the boisterous activity that went on just up the road at Rose Cottage. He'd been a bit of a nerd, far too studious for his own good, and way too much of an introvert to ask to be included in the impromptu gatherings that seemed to be going on all the time whenever the four granddaughters were in town. Besides, those four beautiful girls had drawn admirers from at least two counties. Josh hadn't stood a chance.

He'd matured a lot in the years since then, in both attitude and physique. He'd found a sport he loved—tennis—and a gym he hated but used regularly. A brilliant student, he'd gained confidence in law school, then added to it when he'd been selected for Richmond's most prestigious law firm. Beautiful women no longer intimidated him. Nor did money and power.

Knowing that he could have it all—lovely, well-connected Stephanie Lockport Williams, the money and the power—had somehow been enough. Discovering that he didn't want any of it had been the shocker.

That's why he was here, in fact, to wrestle with himself over how incredibly stupid it might be to throw it all away. He was having far fewer second thoughts today, now that the breakup with Stephanie had gone so smoothly and left him feeling so thoroughly relieved. It had made him wonder if the timing wasn't precisely right for a lot of dramatic changes in his life.

He was up at dawn, anxious to get out on the water, where he could while away the morning fishing…or pretending to. He rushed through breakfast, put away the few clothes he'd brought along, then made a quick call to his folks to let them know he was settled in.

Eventually, armed with bottled water, a sandwich, a

fishing pole and bait, he headed for the bay where it lapped against the shoreline at the back of his family's property. He climbed into the seaworthy old boat at the end of the dock and pushed off. Paddling just far enough away from shore to sustain the pretense that he was at sea, he dropped anchor, cast his line, then leaned back, his old fishing hat pulled low over his eyes.

He was just settling down, content with the warmth of the fall sun against his bare skin, when something crashed into the boat, tilting it precariously and very nearly sending him over the side. The splashing of icy water all over his heated skin was as much a shock as the collision.

Oddly enough, he wasn't all that surprised when he peered over the bow to see Ashley with her face buried in her hands, the paddle floating about three feet away from her kayak.

He couldn't help chuckling at her crestfallen expression. "You know, if you wanted to see me again, all you had to do was call. If you keep ramming into me like this, I'm not going to have any modes of transportation left."

"Obviously I am completely out of control on land or sea," she said in a tone that bore an unexpected edge of hysteria.

Josh stared at her. "Are you okay?"

"Sure. Fine," she said at once, putting on a brave smile to prove it.

She was reasonably convincing, but Josh wasn't buying it. She might be physically fine, but there was something else going on, something that had to do with this vacation she was taking with such obvious reluctance. Her sisters had alluded to it last night.

"Maybe you should come aboard," he suggested, not liking the idea of her being on the water alone when she was obviously shaky. On closer inspection, he thought he detected traces of dried tears on her cheeks. Maybe if he focused on her turmoil, he could put off his own decisions.

"I have my kayak," she protested.

"We can tie it up to the boat." He gestured toward the paddle that was drifting rapidly away. "You won't get far without that paddle, anyway."

"Story of my life lately," she muttered, but she held out her hand to take his, then managed to gingerly climb into the rowboat. "You're very brave, you know."

"For taking you in like this?"

"Exactly. I'm obviously a danger to myself and everyone around me."

"Something tells me that's a relatively new condition," he said, keeping his gaze away from her, hoping she would feel free to tell him what was going on that had her behaving with what he suspected was uncharacteristic carelessness.

"I suppose," she conceded.

To his disappointment, she stopped right there. He decided not to press. Instead he asked, "Know how to bait a hook?"

She regarded him skeptically. "With what?"

"Shrimp."

She nodded. "That's okay, then. If you'd said worms, I'd have jumped overboard and swum home."

"Squeamish, huh?"

"No, absolutely not," she said at once, rising to the challenge with predictable indignation.

"Some sort of animal-rights stance?" he taunted.

A faint flicker of amusement lit her eyes for the first time since they'd met.

"Hardly," she said. "They're just... I guess messy describes it."

"Then I can assume you won't be cleaning any fish we catch for supper?"

"I don't expect to catch any," she said, even as she gingerly dangled the baited hook over the side of the boat, then studied the line with total concentration. After a minute, she glanced at him and asked, "Do you do this every day?"

"Every day I can. I get some of my best thinking done out here on the bay."

"You're not bored?" she asked wistfully.

Josh bit back a grin. Maybe that was the trouble with Ms. Ashley D'Angelo. She didn't know the first thing about relaxing. Even now on this beautiful fall day surrounded by some of the most glorious scenery on earth, she was obviously edgy and uptight.

He studied her intently for a minute, trying not to let his gaze linger on those endless bare legs. He certainly couldn't spot any other flaws. Maybe he could help her work on the relaxation thing.

"I'm never bored," he told her. "I like my own company."

"No significant other?"

"I've been seeing a woman," he admitted. "But I've just recently reached the conclusion that she's not significant. She's a great woman, just not right for me. We broke it off last night."

"Last night?" she asked, obviously startled.

"I called her after I got home from dinner at your sister's."

She seemed to be wrestling with that information. He waited to see if she'd ask if there was a connection, but she didn't.

After studying him with undisguised curiosity, she eventually asked, "How did you conclude that the relationship was over?"

"I was faced with fishing or cutting bait, so to speak. It was time to get married…or not. I couldn't see myself with her forever. Fortunately, as it turned out, she couldn't see that, either."

"Is there something wrong with her?"

"Absolutely not. She's beautiful, intelligent, well-connected. She'll be a dream wife for the right man."

"But not you?"

"Not me," he confirmed.

"If beautiful, intelligent and well-connected aren't right for you, then what kind of woman do you want?"

"I'm still figuring that out," he admitted. "Offhand, though, I'd have to say one who's comfortable in her own skin, someone who knows who she is and what she wants."

"And this woman isn't like that?"

"She is." He shrugged. "But the sparks weren't there. Who knows why that happens? Seems to me that love is just as mysterious as all the philosophers have claimed it is."

She seemed to deflate a little at that. If they hadn't just met, Josh would have said she was actually disappointed.

"That whole bit about being comfortable with who and what you are would definitely let me out," she said a little too brightly.

"Going through an identity crisis?" Josh asked, relieved to finally have something specific to work with to try to figure her out.

"Yes, that's exactly it."

"Welcome to the club."

"You, too?"

Josh nodded. "But I'm not going to worry about it today. Neither should you. Relax and maybe the answers will come to you when your mind's clear of all the clutter."

"Relax?" she said again, as if it were a foreign concept.

Josh chuckled. "Like this," he explained patiently. "Lean back."

He waited until she'd followed his directions. "Okay, then. Now pull the brim of your hat down low to shade your eyes."

She did that, her expression totally serious.

"Now close your eyes and concentrate on the water lapping against the side of the boat," he suggested soothingly. "Feel the sun on your skin."

She sighed. "It feels wonderful."

"There you go. It's all about getting in touch with yourself and letting everything else kind of drift away."

She followed his advice as dutifully as if her life depended on it. He might have been amused, if there had been time. Unfortunately, a fish picked that precise moment to snag Ashley's line, and the next thing he knew he had his arms around her waist and was hanging on for dear life as she tried to reel in the rockfish that was just as determined to get away.

He was all too aware of the soft, sun-kissed scent of her skin, of the way her muscles flexed as she worked the line, of the softness of her breasts against his fore-arm. She was strong and fiercely determined not to be beaten by a fish. In fact, he had to bite his lip to keep from chuckling at the string of curses she muttered when she seemed to be losing the battle.

Only when the rockfish was finally flopping around in a bucket of salt water onboard, did Josh finally dare to meet her gaze. "Competitive, aren't you?"

"You have no idea," she murmured.

Josh nodded slowly. The revelations were coming bit by bit, each one adding to the enigma that was Ashley D'Angelo. Things were definitely going to get very interesting before he had a complete picture of this woman who was so triumphant about landing a fish.

And if the jangling of his pulse right now was any indication, this vacation of his might not turn out to be half as relaxing as he'd imagined.

Chapter Four

"That's three for me," Ashley announced triumphantly as she reeled in her third rockfish of the morning. She grinned at Josh. "And how many for you?"

He laughed, obviously not the least bit intimidated by her success. "None. I haven't had the time. I've been too busy trying to get your fish in the boat without you going overboard. You really need to curb your enthusiasm just a little. A rowboat isn't as stable as, say, a fishing pier. You can't jump around on it."

"That sounds like an excuse to me," Ashley said, enjoying goading him. He refused to take her seriously. She supposed it was that *nice* thing again. He actually seemed happy that she was doing so well and having so much fun. She couldn't recall the last time she'd been around a man who wasn't out to get the better of her.

Maybe that was because most of the men she knew were prosecutors. They tended to be driven, focused and devoid of humor.

"Now what?" she asked Josh, surprisingly eager for more of the kind of lighthearted banter and entertainment he was providing. She hadn't thought about work for several hours now.

"We take them home and clean them," he said. "The person who catches them is definitely responsible for cleaning them."

"I don't think so. I've done all the hard work," she retorted. "We have these fish because of me. I think that makes it your job to clean them."

"Excellent point," he said.

"Thank you," she said modestly.

He held up his hand. "However, and this is important, you did not reel them in entirely on your own. I did help."

Ashley considered his claim. Fairness dictated that she acknowledge his role in the day's catch. "I'll give you that."

"So we clean them together."

She shook her head. "I don't think so."

"How would you suggest we divvy up the labor?"

She thought it over. "You clean 'em. I'll cook 'em. How about that?"

"Can you cook?"

She laughed. He had her there. Maggie was the cook in the family. "At least as well as you can fish," she said eventually. "I'll call Maggie. She's the professional in the kitchen. I'm sure she can coach me through it."

Of course, even as she uttered the words, Ashley knew what a bad idea it was to call her sister in on this.

She'd never hear the end of it. "Better yet, I'll find a cookbook. There's bound to be one at Rose Cottage. If I could pass the bar exam, I'm sure I can follow directions. How hard can it be?"

Josh held out his hand. "Deal."

Ashley accepted his outstretched hand. "Deal," she agreed, as her pulse did a little bump and grind at the contact. Her gaze sought Josh's to see if he'd felt it, as well. With his cap pulled low over his eyes, it was impossible to read anything in his expression.

When they reached the dock at Rose Cottage, he tied up the rowboat, then stepped into the shallow water and secured her kayak.

After helping her from the boat, he picked up the bucket of fish and his cooler and headed for the house. "I'll just put these inside, then head home to get cleaned up. What time do you want to have dinner?"

"Actually I'm starved now," she admitted, surprised to find that it was true. Her stomach was actually growling. It must have something to do with the salt air and exercise. "Much as I appreciated it, that half sandwich you shared with me didn't do the trick."

"Same here. How about I come back in an hour? It shouldn't take me more than fifteen minutes to row back to my place. That'll leave plenty of time for me to shower and drive back. Anything you want me to pick up for dinner?"

Ashley thought about the contents of the refrigerator. She'd brought some things with her, and Maggie had seen to it that it was stocked with plenty of salad ingredients before her arrival. The only thing missing was dessert. Normally she was content with fresh fruit, but the first full day of her vacation seemed to call for something decadent. If nothing else, it might demonstrate that she was starting to view this time-out as something worthy of celebration, rather than as punishment.

"Would you mind going to the bakery if there's time?" she asked.

"Let me guess. You want chocolate," he said, grinning.

"The richest, gooeyest chocolate they have," she confirmed. "Brownies, cake, fudge, mousse—I'm not choosy."

"And if the bakery's closed?"

"Why would it be closed?"

"It's almost five now."

She stared at him in shock. It couldn't be. "We spent the entire day on the water doing nothing?"

He laughed. "Pretty much. You got the knack for relaxing a lot quicker than I expected you to. The nap you took filled an hour or so."

"I did not take a nap," she protested. "I merely closed my eyes for a couple of minutes."

"Whatever. Bottom line, the day has slipped away. Let me get going before any more of it slips by. I'll do my best on the chocolate thing."

She watched him go with an odd feeling in the pit of her stomach. She'd spent an entire day in the company of a man she barely knew, doing something that hadn't exactly taxed her mind, and she hadn't been bored. Not for a single second. Amazing.

She was still pondering that when she went inside and discovered the phone ringing. She debated ignoring it, but realized that would only bring her sisters rushing over here in a panic. She picked it up reluctantly.

"Where the devil have you been?" Maggie demanded at once. "I've been calling for hours. I was beginning to think you'd run back to Boston. Melanie was about to start packing so we could come after you."

"I've been fishing," she responded.

"Excuse me?"

"You know, the activity in which a person puts bait on a hook, puts the hook in the water and reels in a fish. At least that's how it's supposed to work. It turns out I'm pretty good at it. I caught three rockfish."

"Uh-huh," Maggie said, clearly stunned. "When did you learn to fish?"

"Today."

"Who taught you?"

Ah, there was that minefield she'd been dreading. "Josh," she admitted. "I sort of ran into him on the water this morning."

"Ran into him?"

"Literally," she confessed. "I took the kayak out. When I slammed into his rowboat, I lost the paddle. He took me on board his boat."

"As in kidnapped you or offered you refuge?"

"Refuge, I suppose."

"I see. You sound surprisingly upbeat for a woman who has spent the entire day in the company of a man who supposedly annoys you, doing something that you wouldn't have been caught dead doing a week ago."

"Times change."

"And your attitude toward Josh—has that changed, too?"

"I always said he was nice. He just got on my nerves last night at your place."

Maggie laughed. "Oh, this is too good. I'm picking up Melanie and coming over. I want to hear more about this fishing excursion."

"Forget about it," Ashley said emphatically.

"Why?"

"Because Josh is coming back for dinner. I'm cooking the fish."

"You're cooking the fish?" Maggie repeated so skeptically it was insulting.

"Yes, dammit. You could help and just tell me how. It'll save me having to look up a recipe."

"Who's cleaning the fish?" Maggie asked.

"Josh."

"Thank God. For a minute, I thought the world might be coming to an end."

"Stop it. Are you going to help me out here or not, Maggie?"

"Okay, okay. You want simple or fancy?"

"What do you think?" Ashley asked wryly.

"Simple it is. Dredge the fillets in flour, salt and pepper, then fry them in about a quarter inch of oil. Make sure the oil is hot, but not too hot. You don't want to burn the fish."

Ashley jotted the instructions down, even though they seemed foolproof. "How long?"

"Till the flour is golden brown. It shouldn't take more than a couple of minutes on each side, depending on how thick the fillets are."

"And that's all there is to it?" Ashley asked, frowning at the simple directions. "You're not leaving out anything critical, so I'll wind up being totally embarrassed?"

"I would not let you humiliate yourself," Maggie

said, sounding wounded by the suggestion. "This is an easy one, Ash. You'll do fine. What else are you having?"

"Salad, and Josh said he'd pick up something for dessert."

"Chocolate?"

"Yes, if you must know."

"My, my. You don't usually lay into the chocolate until you're really, really comfortable with a man. Or under a lot of stress. Which is it, Ashley?"

"Go suck an egg. Josh is an easygoing guy. It's no big deal. It's not like it's a date or something."

"Really? Not a date? Just out of curiosity, what would you call it?"

"Dinner with a friend."

Maggie chuckled. "Delusional, but nice. Have fun, big sister."

She hung up before Ashley could reassert that her sister was way, way off base.

What was it with women and chocolate? Josh stared indecisively at the display case in the bakery. There was a chocolate layer cake, a chocolate mousse cake, two brownies with icing and walnuts, and eclairs topped with chocolate icing and filled with chocolate cream. They all looked decadent enough to him, but which one would satisfy Ashley? He had a hunch she was very particular.

"Decided yet?" the cheery young clerk asked him.

"Which is your favorite?"

She shrugged. "I like blueberry pie myself."

Obviously she was going to be no help at all. He finally gave up in frustration. "I'll take it all."

Her jaw dropped. "Are you having a party or something?"

"Not really." He was pretty sure dinner with Ashley didn't qualify as a party. He doubted she even saw it as a date.

To be honest, he hadn't quite decided what this evening was all about, either. He just knew that he'd rushed like crazy to get ready to go to Rose Cottage. Being invited there by one of the D'Angelo sisters was like a dream come true. Despite all the strides he'd made in building his self-confidence over the years, he still couldn't quite believe it. He felt like the shy, awkward boy he'd been at sixteen. He wanted to get this right.

He paid the disbelieving clerk for the boxes of desserts, then headed the few miles back to Rose Cottage.

When Ashley opened the door, he almost swallowed his tongue. She was wearing a thin robe that clung to her still damp body, revealing every intriguing shadow, every lush curve. Her hair was in damp ringlets that sprang free from some sort of scrunchy thing that was supposed to be holding it on top of her head.

"Sorry," she said, sounding frantic. "I had a phone call right after you left. It took me longer to get started in the shower than I expected. Make yourself at home. Get whatever you need in the kitchen to clean the fish. I'll be down in a minute."

She bolted for the stairs without waiting for a reply. Just as well, Josh thought, since it took him fully a minute to get the blood flowing back to his brain where it was necessary for speech.

"Clean the fish," he muttered as he set out to find the kitchen. "Just concentrate on cleaning the fish." Maybe that would drive the provocative image of Ashley in that revealing robe out of his head before she came back downstairs.

He was out back, scraping the scales from the last fish, when she finally emerged from the house. Thankfully, she was wearing loose jeans and a shapeless T-shirt, which looked as if they'd been borrowed from someone two sizes larger. Even so, she managed to stir his blood. Apparently she was going to do that no matter what she wore, he concluded. He'd just have to resign himself to it.

She'd dried her tawny hair into waves that fell to her shoulders. Her skin was clear and free of makeup, except for the faintest pink gloss on her lips. Even with all the suntan lotion she'd lathered on while they were on the water, her color was heightened to a healthy pink glow. She looked a thousand-percent better than the pale, shaken woman he'd met the day before.

"How's it coming out here?" she asked.

"Just about finished. Have you figured out how to cook them?"

"Rest easy," she said. "My sister has coached me through it. We probably won't die of food poisoning." She regarded him with apparent amusement. "By the way, why are there four bakery boxes on the kitchen table?"

He shrugged. "I couldn't make up my mind what you'd like best."

"So you bought out the place?"

"Pretty much—at least everything chocolate," he admitted. "You don't have to eat it all."

"But I probably will," she admitted with a sigh. "Chocolate is what gets me through stress."

"And you're stressed now?" he asked.

She hesitated, then regarded him with surprise. "Not right this second, no."

He grinned. "I told you there were advantages to a day in a rowboat."

"Apparently so. I haven't thought about work all day long. That's like some sort of miracle."

"Then let's keep that track record intact and get dinner on the table."

Ashley nodded at once. "Good plan. If I start to bring up anything work-related over dinner, cut me off."

Josh wasn't sure he'd be able to agree to that indefinitely, but he could for tonight. "No work. Got it."

In the kitchen, they worked side-by-side. He made the salad while she fried the fish. When the plates were ready, they sat at the kitchen table and Ashley lifted a glass of wine in a toast.

"To relaxation," she said.

"It's a wonderful thing," Josh added.

"Even if it can't last forever," she said, looking just a little sad.

"Hey, that borders on mentioning work," he scolded. "Maybe we need to have a penalty."

Competitive woman that she was, Ashley immediately seized on the idea, just as he'd known she would.

"Such as?" she asked at once.

"We each have a pot and put in a dollar for every infraction. We're on the honor system. We have to put the money in even if the other person isn't around. At the end of the week, the one with the fewest violations gets all the money." He grinned. "And gets treated to dinner by the loser."

She considered the scheme thoughtfully, as if weighing her odds of winning. "I can do that," she said finally.

Josh doubted it, but he lifted his glass. "To relaxation," he toasted one more time.

They'd no sooner taken a sip than his cell phone rang. He could have sworn he'd left it turned off on his dresser, but apparently it had been stuck in the pocket of his jacket.

"Aren't you going to get that?" Ashley asked.

He debated the wisdom of it, then finally reached for his jacket and grabbed it out of the pocket. "Yes?"

"Have you lost your mind, Madison?"

"Mr. Williams," he said, barely containing a sigh.

"I've spoken to Stephanie," his boss said. "She tells me the two of you have called off your engagement."

Josh barely clung to his temper. "We were never engaged, sir."

"Semantics. We all knew you were headed in that direction."

"You were the only one who really believed that," Josh corrected. "Fortunately Stephanie and I realized before it was too late that it would be a mistake. Look, sir, this isn't really a good time. Perhaps we can discuss this later."

"Now's good for me," Creighton Williams insisted. "You realize what this is going to do to your future here at Brevard, Williams and Davenport, don't you?"

"I assume it's over. If so, that's fine."

His ready acceptance of the end of his career clearly caught his boss off guard. "Now let's not be hasty, Madison. You're a good lawyer. This might get you off that fast track, but I don't want to lose you over this. Besides,

Stephanie made it clear she'd be furious if I fired you. We'll work something out when you get back."

"That's very generous of you, sir, but I'll have to get back to you on that."

"What the devil are you saying?"

He finally risked a look at Ashley and noted that she was listening avidly to every word. "I'm saying that I'm on vacation. We'll discuss it another time. Thanks for calling. I mean that, sir. It was very gracious of you."

He shut the phone off completely and barely resisted the urge to toss it out the back door. He waited for the litany of questions to begin.

"Go ahead, ask," he said finally.

She grinned. "That was about work, right?"

He nodded, uncertain where she was going. It didn't seem to be in the direction he'd expected.

Ashley held up a slip of paper with little marks on it. "I counted half a dozen references to work, minimum. That's six dollars in your pot, please."

Josh fought a laugh. "You counted that conversation in our bet?"

"Of course. We had a deal. We sealed it with a toast before the phone rang."

"Oh, brother, you must be hell on wheels in a courtroom."

She grinned. "That's another one. Seven dollars."

He frowned at her. "Dammit, I was referring to *your* work, not mine."

"Did we differentiate?" she inquired sweetly.

He sighed. "No, we did not differentiate. This is going to be a lot trickier than I expected."

"Which means we should probably change the subject, even though I'm winning," Ashley conceded with a magnanimous air. "Do you know anything about baseball? I'm a Red Sox fan myself."

Josh stared at her, not entirely sure if she was serious. "Really? When was the last time you went to a baseball game?"

She faltered a bit at that. "I don't actually go to the games," she confessed eventually. "That doesn't mean I don't follow the team."

"Then you watch them on TV?"

"Not really."

"Read the sports pages?" he asked, his amusement growing.

"Okay, okay, I don't know a damn thing about baseball," she finally said. "But people in the office mention it. Obviously it's something some people care about. I thought you might be one of them. I was just trying to make conversation."

Josh grinned and held out his hand. "I'll take a dollar, please. You mentioned your office."

She stared at him with apparent dismay. "That doesn't count."

"Of course it does. Office, work, it's all the same thing."

"Oh, for heaven's sakes," she muttered, as she dug in her purse and tossed a dollar onto the table. "I'm still winning."

"And we have a week to go. Don't get overly confident, sweetheart. It's unbecoming."

She frowned at him. "Seen any good movies lately?"

"Not a one. You?"

"No."

"Read any good books?" he asked, fully expecting her to slip up and make some reference to a law journal.

Her expression brightened. "Actually, I read a great one yesterday afternoon. It almost made me late for dinner."

"Would I like it?"

"I doubt it. It was a love story."

"Hey, I'm all in favor of love."

She regarded him with blatant skepticism. "You want to read this?"

"Sure, why not? The fish was very good, by the way. You follow directions well."

She seemed startled by the praise. Her gaze shifted to his clean plate, then to her own. "I do, don't I? Maybe I'll learn to cook while I'm here."

"I'd be happy to be your guinea pig," he offered. "I have a cast-iron stomach. I have to, given how lousy I am in the kitchen."

"Maybe Maggie could give us both lessons," she suggested. "That could be fun."

"Even relaxing," he retorted. "As long as you don't turn it into some sort of competition."

"Not everything has to be a competition with me," she insisted.

"Really? I'll bet by the time you were three, you wanted to know if your hands were the cleanest when you came to the supper table."

"I did not," she said, but there was a spark of recognition in her eyes that suggested she saw herself in his comment just the same.

Josh wondered if a woman who obviously thrived on challenges would ever be content with a slower, less stressful pace, or if she would always need to be in the thick of some battle. It was something he needed to decide about himself, as well.

He'd come down here to simplify his life, to cut through the clutter of being on the fast track and see if he wanted to get off entirely. He suspected Ashley wasn't in the same place at all. If anything, she was probably champing at the bit to get back on that fast track. It might be the kind of complication that meant they were doomed, but it was hardly something that needed to be resolved tonight.

Tonight it was enough to be with a woman who stirred his blood and kept him on his toes mentally. At some point during the evening, he'd gotten past the triumph of being invited to Rose Cottage by one of the unattainable D'Angelo sisters. Now it was all about being with a woman who intrigued him, a woman with strengths and vulnerabilities he wanted to understand, a woman whose bed he wanted to share.

When that thought cavorted through his head, he immediately slammed on the brakes. He was getting ahead of himself, way ahead of himself.

He glanced across the table and saw Ashley studying him intently. There was an unmistakable and totally unexpected hunger in her eyes. He told himself it had to be for the chocolate.

"Ready for dessert?" he asked, his voice thick and unsteady.

She nodded, her gaze never leaving his.

"Cake?"

She shook her head.

"A brownie?"

Again, that subtle shake.

Josh swallowed hard. "Eclair?"

"Not right now."

"What do you want?"

"You," she said quietly.

Amazement flooded through him. "But—"

"No questions, no doubts, unless you don't want me," she said.

"That is definitely not the issue," he admitted.

Her lips curved slightly. "Then why are you still sitting there?"

"Because I'm an idiot," he said, trying to ignore the way his pulse was racing with anticipation. He *was* a nice guy, dammit, and she was vulnerable. He would not take advantage of her.

She stared at him for an eternity. "You're saying no?"

He nodded. "I don't know what brought you down here, but having sex with me isn't the answer."

"It could be the answer tonight," she said lightly.

He smiled at that. "Indeed, it could be spectacular, but when you and I get together for the first time—and we will, Ashley—then I want it to be because it's inevitable, not because it's convenient."

Patches of red flared in her cheeks. "I'm sorry. I'm the idiot," she said, instantly stiff and unapproachable again.

"Don't you dare say that," he chided. "You have no idea how flattered I am that you suggested this or how hard it was for me to say no. We'll get around to making love, make no mistake about that."

"I'm only here for three weeks," she reminded him, as if to define the urgency.

He grinned. "Which means we still have twenty days

left. Since we barely got through one without tumbling straight into your bed, I suspect we won't waste too many."

She stared at him quizzically, as if she were trying to discover if he was making fun of her. Apparently she recognized just how serious he was, because she laughed. The tension evaporated.

But Josh knew that thanks to his noble gesture, sleep was going to be a very long time coming.

Chapter Five

Ashley still felt like a first-class idiot in the morning. Josh had been amazingly gracious when she'd hit on him, but she'd clearly misread all the signals. She'd thought all those sparks were going to lead to something that would help her to forget her problems. Fishing, pleasant as it had been, sure as hell wasn't going to do that. A steamy, meaningless affair might have.

Oh, well, no one died of acute humiliation. She simply wouldn't make that mistake again. For all she knew, Josh wouldn't even set foot on the grounds at Rose Cottage again, despite all those pretty words and promises.

She was still beating herself up as she lingered over her second cup of coffee when someone knocked on the kitchen door, then walked right in. She glanced up, fully expecting it to be her sisters, only to find Josh there in another pair of faded shorts and another of those equally disreputable T-shirts. He looked incredible. Her resolve to forget about an affair sizzled and died.

Without saying a word, he walked over to the table, leaned down and kissed her. The first touch of his lips on hers was a shock. She had a hunch he'd meant it to be nothing more than a casual, good-morning kind of kiss, but it set off enough heat to boil eggs. Her head was spinning, and she was pretty sure her eyes had to be crossed by the time he pulled away. If he'd been trying to prove that he'd meant what he said the night before, he'd accomplished that and then some.

"I thought you might be over here beating yourself up about trying to seduce me last night," he said as he casually turned to the coffeepot and poured himself the last cup. She'd drunk all the rest of the coffee herself.

Indignation flared at his comment, even though he'd guessed exactly right. "So what? You decided to come over and toss me a consolation prize?"

He laughed. "No, I came over to prove that you have nothing to worry about. A couple more kisses like that one and I won't be able to resist you. My noble intentions will fly right out the window."

She frowned at him. "Was that my mistake last night—not grabbing you and kissing you right off the bat?"

"You didn't make any mistakes last night," he assured her. "Aside from being a little premature." He surveyed her. "Why aren't you dressed for fishing?"

"I didn't know we were going fishing," she said, her tone still peevish. He'd thrown her completely off-kilter yet again. It was getting to be an annoying habit. The men she liked were predictable. None of them would have turned down her offer of uncomplicated sex.

And, she was forced to admit, none of them would have been back here this morning suggesting a fishing trip.

"You have something else planned?" he asked.

She shook her head.

"Then let's get a move on. Those fish won't wait forever."

She grinned despite herself. "I thought the object was to relax, that actually catching a fish didn't really matter."

"It doesn't to me," he said indifferently, then winked. "But you seem to need immediate gratification."

"Is that an insult?"

He laughed. "Nope, just an observation. We're going to work on that."

"What if I don't want to change?" she asked curiously.

"Then it will be more of a struggle than I'm expecting," he said easily. "Go, put on a swimsuit under your clothes. Maybe I'll let you race me to the dock later."

"Will you let me win?"

"Not a chance."

Ashley laughed. "Now you've really made it interesting. I'll be right back."

Upstairs, she pulled on her prim, one-piece bathing suit, then added a T-shirt, shorts and a pair of dingy sneakers she hadn't worn since college. She grabbed her cap from the day before and a bottle of suntan lotion. She hesitated in the bedroom doorway as if she were forgetting something, then realized that going fishing didn't require a tenth of the paraphernalia she took with her to work each day. It was actually a relief to go downstairs without a purse or briefcase weighing her down.

She took the keys from a peg on the wall, then announced, "I'm ready."

Josh grinned. "Love the shoes. They make a statement."

She glanced pointedly at his faded and misshapen boat shoes. "It's not as if you just stepped out of a designer shoe showroom."

"Hey, don't you dare insult these old things. They're just getting comfortable."

They'd barely stepped out the back door, still bantering, when Melanie and Maggie rounded the corner of the house. Ashley's good humor vanished in a heartbeat. She muttered a curse, ruing the day she'd ever interfered in her sisters' lives, since they now seemed to feel totally free to butt into hers.

"We heard that," Maggie scolded. "Is that any way to welcome your loving sisters who've come to check on you?"

"As if that's why you're here," she retorted. "You're here to spy."

"Which would hardly matter if you have nothing to hide," Melanie commented, her gaze on Josh. "Been here long?" she asked him.

"A few minutes," Ashley responded emphatically.

"Then this is like a second date or something," Maggie said. "Fascinating."

"It's not a date," Ashley said automatically. "We're going fishing."

"Oh, yes, fishing," Maggie repeated, amusement threading through her voice. "I forgot that doesn't count. If it did, that would actually make this the third date, since you went fishing yesterday, too, isn't that right, Josh?"

He regarded her with undisguised reluctance. "Don't

ask me. I'm staying out of this one. You ladies work it out. Me, I'm not much on labels. I'm a go-with-the-flow kind of guy."

Ashley frowned at him. "You are not. Otherwise—"

He interrupted, grinning at her. "Do you really want to go there?"

Ashley sighed and shut up.

"Smart and handsome," Melanie said with approval.

"A dead man," Ashley commented, scowling at him. "You were supposed to back me up. We're not dating."

"Oh, I must have missed that memo." He dutifully turned to her sisters. "We're not dating."

"Then what are you doing?" Maggie inquired sweetly. "Besides kissing, that is?"

"Kissing?" Ashley asked. "Where would you get an idea like that?"

"The clues are everywhere," Maggie said blithely. "Those telltale traces of lipstick on Josh's face, for instance, and the fact that your lipstick is the exact same shade… What's left of it, anyway."

Ashley felt her cheeks flaming. She turned to Josh. "Have I mentioned that my sisters are a couple of obnoxious meddlers?"

"I think it's sweet," he said.

"Sweet?" she echoed incredulously. "What's sweet about them barging in here and making you uncomfortable?"

"I'm not uncomfortable."

She stared at him. He did seem perfectly at ease. She was the only one about to jump out of her skin. "Oh, forget it. I'm going fishing. The rest of you can do whatever the hell you want to do."

"Sorry, ladies," Josh said. "I think that's my cue. Have a nice day."

They were in the boat before Ashley finally risked a look into his eyes. They were sparkling with amusement.

"You thought that was funny, didn't you?" she demanded irritably.

"I don't know about funny, but it wasn't quite the big deal you want to turn it into."

"Just wait," she muttered direly. "Just you wait."

She was going to take a certain amount of perverse pleasure in watching Josh squirm when her sisters decided he was exactly the right catch and set out to reel him in for her.

Josh recalled Ashley's warning when he was sitting in a booth at a café later that afternoon with a cappuccino and the Richmond paper and he spotted Maggie and Melanie about to descend on him. They looked as thrilled as if they'd just noticed an especially plump turkey for their Thanksgiving dinner.

"Hello again," Maggie said, sliding into the booth opposite him.

Melanie slipped in beside him, so there would be no escape. "Where's Ashley?"

"I dropped her back at Rose Cottage about an hour ago."

"Catch any fish today?" Maggie asked.

"Not a one," he admitted, recalling just how frustrating that had been to Ashley. She hadn't quite gotten the knack of appreciating the process more than the outcome. She'd been very irritable when he'd left her at Rose Cottage.

Melanie laughed. "Uh-oh, that must have driven Ashley up a wall. She probably took it as a personal affront."

"Pretty much," he agreed. In fact, she'd made such a commotion, it was little wonder the fish had taken off. He hadn't had the nerve to point out to her that fish tended to flee when humans made too much racket.

Maggie's gaze narrowed. "Did that make you run for cover?"

"No, it made me run home to change into clean clothes so I could meet her here for coffee."

"Oh," Maggie said, obviously deflated.

"Do you honestly want to be here cross-examining me when she gets here?" he inquired.

The two women exchanged a look. "Probably a bad idea," Melanie admitted.

"She'll think we're spying again," Maggie agreed. "But we have our eyes on you, Madison. Don't forget that."

Josh laughed. "Not for a minute," he promised.

Maggie gave him one last considering look. "You could be good for her."

"Thank you."

"Has she told you why she's hiding out down here?"

"No."

"Make her tell you," she urged. "She needs to talk about it."

"Maybe what she needs is to put it behind her," Josh suggested. "Sometimes you can talk a thing to death."

"Nice theory, but talking things to death is how Ashley handles a crisis," Maggie informed him. "This time she's clammed up. It's not healthy."

"I don't suppose you want to share a little information with me, maybe tell me what it is I'm supposed to get her to talk about," he suggested.

"Sorry," Maggie said. "She'd kill us if we told."

"Does it have something to do with work?"

They exchanged a look, then nodded.

"Then we have a problem. She and I have agreed to avoid the subject of work at all costs. In fact we have a bet going about who can do the best job of steering clear of the topic."

"Great, that's just great," Maggie said in obvious disgust, oblivious to the suddenly frantic signals Melanie was trying to send her.

"Actually it *is* great," Ashley chimed in, startling Maggie. "Work is not a topic I care to get into with anyone right now, including the two of you. Go away." She frowned at Josh. "Didn't I warn you about them?"

"Hey, I was sitting here minding my own business and they turned up. It's not like I invited them to join us."

Maggie's expression brightened. "What a good idea! We'd love to."

"It is *not* a good idea," Ashley said emphatically. "Go away. If you don't, I will."

"Okay, fine," Maggie said as she and Melanie stood up. "We'll leave you in Josh's capable hands." She turned to him. "Remember our advice. And forget about that stupid bet."

Ashley stood watching them until they were out the door. Then she sat down opposite him. "What advice did they give you?"

"They think I need to ask you about what drove you down here," he said. He searched her face, watching for a reaction. She managed to keep her expression totally neutral. "Do I?"

"Absolutely not. I don't want to talk about it," she said fiercely.

He sighed. "Which tells me it is exactly what we need to discuss."

She regarded him plaintively. "Why?"

"Because it's apparently the key to getting to know who you are."

"You know who I am."

"I know what you've allowed me to see. It's all pretty superficial, Ashley."

She gave him a sour look. "Am I boring you?"

"Hardly."

"Then think of it this way—there are layers and layers yet to be peeled away. One of these days I may let you get started on that, but not now, okay?"

"You can't solve problems if you hide from them," he commented. Not that he was a sterling example of someone who paid attention to that particular advice. Wasn't he as guilty of avoiding things at the moment as she was? He hadn't given one moment's thought to his future once he'd resolved things with Stephanie. He was letting it all percolate on the back burner in the hope that things would work themselves out eventually without any effort on his part.

Ashley frowned at the unsolicited advice. "I can only learn one new trick at a time. I'm still having trouble with the relaxation thing. This other business would pretty much set me back by a month."

Josh laughed. "Okay, okay. We'll stick to relaxing for now. And speaking of that, what would you like? I could use another cappuccino. I'll go up to the counter and order."

"A cappuccino sounds good," she said. "I'll look at the paper till you get back."

It didn't take Josh more than five minutes to order their coffee and take the drinks back to the table, but something had obviously happened while he was away. Every bit of color had washed out of Ashley's face, and she was clutching a balled up chunk of newsprint in her fist.

"Ashley?" he asked, scooting into the booth next to her. "What is it?"

She shook her head, looking dazed.

Josh tried to pry the paper from her hand, but she refused to release it. He racked his brain trying to recall anything that had been in the paper that might have had this obviously devastating effect on her, but nothing came to him. Besides, she had no ties to Richmond that he knew of.

"Talk to me, sweetheart. Something's obviously upset you."

"I can't," she whispered, her voice choked. "Let me out of here. I think I'm going to be sick."

She ran from the café with Josh hard on her heels. He caught her at the corner. She was bending over, holding her stomach, gasping for breath. He rubbed her back, murmuring soothing nonsense, until she finally shuddered and turned to him, burying her face against his shoulder. He'd never before in his life seen anyone with such a stricken look in their eyes. It made him want to kill whoever was responsible for putting it there.

"Tell me, please," he pleaded. "I can't help if I don't know what's going on."

"Can we take a break from the bet?" she asked.

Josh almost laughed that she would think of their bet at a time like this. "Okay, we're on a time-out," he assured her. "Now tell me."

She lifted her gaze to his, her expression drained. Finally she seemed to reach some sort of conclusion because she held out her hand and let him take the piece of newspaper.

Josh smoothed it out as best he could with one hand, while still keeping one arm firmly around her waist. He had a feeling she needed the contact far more than he needed to get immediate answers.

The first side of the page was nothing but part of an ad for a Richmond department store. When he turned it over, he saw that it was from a column of national news briefs. The dateline was Boston.

Freed Killer Strikes Again, the headline stated. He glanced at Ashley's face. There was guilt and shame in her expression as if she were somehow responsible.

"What do you know about this?" he asked quietly.

"I know that man," she said after what seemed like an eternity. "I represented him at his last trial for murder. I just got him off a week ago. My firm's still representing him."

Oh, dear God in heaven, Josh thought, his heart aching for her. *That* was what had brought her to Rose Cottage, the knowledge that she had helped to free a murderer. And now the man had almost killed again. Only quick police intervention had stopped him. It would devastate any lawyer, but especially one who took such evident pride in her courtroom skills. She'd obviously been duped by the man into believing in his innocence. She wouldn't be the first lawyer to be fooled, or the last, but she obviously held herself to exceedingly high standards.

"It's not your fault," he said firmly.

"Of course it is. That disgusting creature wouldn't have been back on the streets if it hadn't been for me. Maybe I didn't know he was guilty when I defended him, but I should have seen it. He would have been in jail now if I hadn't been so aggressive in that courtroom."

"Was the prosecution's case airtight?"

"No," she admitted. "The forensics evidence was sloppy as hell."

"Did you do anything unethical?"

"No."

"Did you follow the law?"

"To the letter."

"Then it wasn't your fault," he repeated. "Remember, our legal system is based on the principle that it's preferable for ten guilty people to go free than for one innocent person to be convicted. The jury is instructed not to convict if there is reasonable doubt, and it's up to the prosecutor to remove that doubt from the jurors' minds."

"Justice wasn't served," she insisted. "Not even close. I have a reputation for picking my cases very carefully. I blew this one."

Josh couldn't argue with that. He knew all too well how cases could sometimes be won or lost not on the evidence, but based on the comparative skills of the lawyers involved. It was one of the reasons he was questioning his own commitment to the law. Maybe now was the time to tell Ashley that, to commiserate with her in a way that told her he really did understand. Somehow, though, he couldn't bring himself to do it. This was about her feelings, and he didn't want to divert the conversation away from that for even a moment.

"I'm sorry," he said softly. "I know how this case must eat at you. My saying it's not your fault doesn't really help. You have to get there on your own."

"I don't know if I ever will." She eyed the article he was holding as if it were a serpent. "Especially now. I'll never be able to practice in Boston again."

"Of course you will," he said. "If that's what you want to do. Good people, honest people, innocent people, get accused of crimes, and they're going to want an attorney who fights with passion and conviction on their side. Those are the ones you'll help."

She regarded him with a sad expression. "But don't you see, Josh? I can't tell the difference."

The misery in her eyes and the hopelessness in her voice were enough to break his heart.

"Of course you can," he assured her. "It's one mistake, Ashley. That doesn't render you incompetent."

"Another person nearly died because of me," she insisted fiercely. "If the police hadn't had him under surveillance..." She shuddered at what could have happened. "I'm as guilty as Tiny Slocum."

"I know that's how you must feel, but you'll see it differently in time," he said, wondering even as he spoke if that were really true. Ashley clearly had a conscience that ran deep. It was one of the most admirable things about her. How would she ever be able to reconcile what had happened with her vision of justice? With her vision of herself?

Worse, he knew that there wasn't a damn thing he could say that would set her mind at ease.

Chapter Six

"You can go now," Ashley told Josh after he'd fixed them both dinner, then sat there patiently, his gaze unrelenting, until she'd eaten almost every bite. His presence, undemanding though it was, was wearing on her nerves. Sooner or later, he was going to insist she talk about Tiny Slocum.

Right now, though, he merely grinned. "Trying to run me off before I make you finish your peas?"

"You caught me," she admitted, trying to match his light tone. "I hate peas."

He gave her a perplexed look. "Then why were there six cans of them in the cupboard?"

"Because Melanie was here first and she stocked the cupboards. She loves peas." Ashley grinned halfheartedly. "Maggie won't touch them, either. Maybe I should consider wrapping them up and giving them to Melanie for Christmas."

Even as she spoke, there was a semi-hysterical note in her voice as she realized that it was entirely possible that she could still be here at Christmas, that her firm might not want her back after all, now that her sterling reputation for being on the side of the angels had been tarnished. Her three-week break, which she'd barely become resigned to, could turn into months of unemployment and indecision.

Given that realization along with everything else, it was a miracle that she could find anything at all to joke about. Ever since she'd seen that news brief in the paper, she'd felt as if all the air had been sucked from her lungs. She hadn't said a dozen words all during dinner. It was little wonder that Josh was reluctant to leave her, even though he had to have lost respect for her, knowing how badly she'd been deluded in the Tiny Slocum case. She was sure Josh would bolt the instant he thought she was calm enough to be left alone. That would be that, the end of a budding…what? Friendship? Relationship?

She regarded him thoughtfully. "Why haven't you run for the hills by now?" Maybe the answer to that would tell her what she needed to know. Maybe it would help her to define whatever was going on between them. She liked everything in her life sorted into nice, neat cubbyholes. Up till now Josh had defied all her attempts at categorization.

But rather than giving her the direct, uncomplicated answer she'd hoped for, he regarded her blankly. "Why would I do that?"

"You've seen unmistakable evidence that I'm a terrible judge of character," she explained. "That might be okay for the average person, but it's a lousy trait for an attorney. *I* don't even have any respect for me anymore."

"Come on, Ashley. I'm not about to confuse a mistake you made with who you are," he told her. "You're a good, decent person."

"You haven't known me long enough to be sure of that," she protested, determined not to listen to anything positive when she was mired in this down-on-herself mood.

"It's *obvious,*" he contradicted just emphatically. "Otherwise this wouldn't be tearing you up the way it is. You'd chalk it up to experience and move right on."

She stared at him in shock. "How could I do that? How could anyone?"

"Attorneys do it all the time," he insisted. "They passionately defend people they know or suspect to be guilty because that's their job. You said yourself that someone at your firm took over Slocum's defense."

"You don't seem to have a very high opinion of lawyers," she observed.

"Just a realistic one, quite possibly a better one than you do at the moment," he said, then waved her off when she would have interrupted. "Let me finish."

"Fine. Go right ahead."

"Maybe a good attorney will try to encourage a plea bargain if the evidence is overwhelming, but ultimately his duty is to act in the best interest of his client, guilty or innocent, and to offer that client the competent defense that is the client's constitutional right, correct?"

"Yes," she admitted.

"You thought you were defending an innocent man. It turned out you were wrong. It's not the same thing as deliberately setting out to free a guilty man."

Ashley refused to be placated. "It feels like the same thing. It feels as if I'm as responsible as Tiny Slocum was when he beat up yet another woman."

Josh looked her in the eye. "How do you think the jurors who acquitted him are feeling right now? Do you blame them? Do you think you duped them?"

She closed her eyes and sighed. "No, not deliberately. Tiny fooled all of us. I'm sure they're as sick at heart as I am."

"Add in the fact that the prosecutor and police messed up. Seems to me as if there's plenty of blame to go around. You don't need to take it all onto your shoulders." He scooted his chair closer and skimmed a finger along her bare arm. "And lovely shoulders they are, too. Much too lovely to have all this weight heaped on them."

Ashley shuddered at his touch. It would be so easy to allow him to distract her, just for a little while. It would be wonderful to have his mouth on hers, his hands exploring her body, to feel him inside her, to give in to sensation, to let him take her hard and fast until she came apart. It was exactly what she'd wanted last night, and it was even more appealing now.

But she wouldn't ask him to stay, not again. Her pride wouldn't allow it, even if her common sense wasn't telling her that the timing was no more right tonight than it had been the night before. If anything, it was worse. They would both know she was only using him to forget her troubles. That was a truly lousy thing to do to a man who'd been nothing but thoughtful and supportive.

She grabbed Josh's hand and pressed a kiss to his knuckles. "You should go," she said quietly. "I need some time to think about all this."

"I'm not so sure you should be alone," he said, his expression uneasy. "If you don't want me here, how about calling one of your sisters?"

She shook her head. "Maggie and Melanie have already listened to me moan and groan enough about all this. They came straight up to Boston to get me after the trial. If you think I'm in bad shape now, you should have seen me then. I was totally impossible and unreasonable. They threatened to have me committed if I didn't take some time off."

"Really? Good for them."

She frowned at him. "Don't tell me you're a proponent of the tough love approach, too."

"I'm a proponent of love in all its forms," he retorted genially. "Now let me do these dishes, and I'll get out from underfoot."

"Josh, I don't think I'm so shaken that I can't wash a few dishes. Doing something totally mundane and mindless will be good for me," she said, anxious for him to be gone before she changed her mind and threw herself at him.

"If you say so," he replied.

"Go. Do something fun and don't spend one second worrying about me. I promise I'll be here in the morning, bright-eyed and ready to go fishing."

He studied her intently for a moment, then nodded. "Okay, then, you win. I'm out of here. Call me if you change your mind and decide you need company. It doesn't matter what time it is. I'm not on any sort of schedule right now. I can be back here in a few minutes."

"I will," she promised.

He leaned down and gave her a hard kiss that stirred regret that she'd already decided to send him on his way.

"Just something else for you to think about," he teased lightly. "I don't want you wasting your whole night on useless guilt."

After he'd gone, Ashley touched her lips. It had been a helluva tactic. As stressed-out as she was about things in Boston, there was a whole lot going on right here to give her pause. One of these days she'd have to figure out why she was so attracted to a man who seemed to have an endless supply of time on his hands and no noticeable goals that she'd been able to discern.

Josh wasn't happy about leaving Ashley alone, but the stubborn set of her jaw had told him she wasn't going to give him any alternative. Better to go gracefully than add to her stress by digging in his heels and staying put. Besides, he had some thinking of his own to do. Maybe this was the perfect opportunity. Ironically the questions plaguing Ashley were not that much of a stretch from those bothering him.

Not that he'd gotten a murderer off recently. He swam in a different legal pond, mostly with the corporate barracudas. It was cutthroat law of a different kind, and he'd pretty much concluded months ago that he wasn't suited for it. He was always hired to represent one side, but he was too damn good at seeing both sides of the picture, especially in some of the high-stakes mergers and acquisitions he handled. His evenhanded judgment made it a lot harder to go for the jugular, even when that was precisely what he was being paid to do.

People who hired Brevard, Williams and Davenport could pay for the best representation available. More and more lately, Josh had wanted to be on the side of the little guy who couldn't afford the big guns. Maybe this was his chance to do just that. He had no financial obligations, no family to consider. If he was ever going to dramatically alter his income and lifestyle, now was the time.

A part of him wanted to go back to Ashley's and bat the whole idea around with her for a while. He had a hunch she would bring a unique perspective to the picture. Maybe it would even help her wrestle with her own dilemma. They could be sounding boards for each other, at least once she got over the shock of discovering that he was one of those lawyers she thought he held in such disdain.

He sighed and dismissed the idea. Ashley didn't want a sounding board right now. She wanted to hibernate and lick her wounds. He honestly couldn't blame her. He'd give her tonight to do that, but come morning, he was going to be back over there and was going to insist they talk her situation out some more, especially if she was still neck-deep in guilt.

"You look like a man with a lot on his mind." Mike startled Josh out of his reverie when he found Josh still sitting behind the wheel of his car in his driveway after he'd driven home from Ashley's.

"Just thinking about this and that," Josh said, climbing out of the car and plastering a fake smile of welcome on his face. "What are you doing here?"

"Actually I was out for a walk and saw your car turn in. I decided I'd stop by and see if you wanted a little company. Melanie and Jessie went shopping for school supplies so I'm at loose ends."

Josh grinned at the restless note in Mike's voice. "Is that what marriage does to you, makes you incapable of being on your own for a few hours?"

Mike laughed. "Pretty much. I'm still shocked by that myself." He gave Josh a speculative look. "You're on your own pretty early, too. Did Ashley kick you out?"

"She had some things she needed to think through," he said, careful not to allude to what those things were. If she didn't want her family to know, it wasn't up to him to spill the beans.

"About your relationship?" Mike prodded.

"No way. To hear her tell it, we don't have a relationship."

"I see. What's your take on that?"

Josh gave the question some serious thought. He liked her, no question about that. He was attracted to her. Definitely no question about that, either. Did they have a future? How could he possibly answer that when neither of them had a clue what they really wanted for the rest of their lives, professionally speaking, anyway? He settled for giving a reply that was honest as far as it went.

"I think that depends on how determined she is to go back to Boston," he told Mike. "There's not much chance of having a relationship with someone whose life is hundreds of miles away."

Mike didn't seem convinced. "You hear about long-distance relationships working all the time. They're tough, but it can be done if both people are committed to it."

"I think it's a little soon for either of us to be thinking about commitment. We barely know each other."

"Sometimes the whole lightning-bolt thing happens," Mike reminded him. "It happened that way for me and Melanie. Same thing with Rick and Maggie. Maybe it's the way things go with the D'Angelo women."

Josh thought of how connected he sometimes felt to Ashley, far more connected than he'd ever felt to Stephanie, despite having known Stephanie so much longer. Maybe Mike was right. Maybe time had nothing to do with love. Still, for a plodder like him, it seemed wrong to be thinking of jumping from thoughts of an eventual engagement to a certain woman one day, to a full-throttle relationship with another woman a few days later. A full-throttle affair, maybe, but he'd already vetoed that idea.

"Let's not jump the gun," he told Mike. "I don't think Ashley's in the best place to be worrying about a relationship with anyone right now."

Mike regarded him with pity. "A word of advice, don't wait for her to decide or to be in the right place. If you want her, let her know it. If you want her to stay here, then pull out the big guns and persuade her to stay. If she's anything like her sisters, this area is in her blood just as much as Boston is, but it might take a little push to help her realize that."

Josh nodded. "I'll keep that in mind. Now how about a beer?" he suggested, anxious to change the subject. "We can swap lies and gossip about everyone we know except the D'Angelo women."

Mike laughed. "Total avoidance. It's a great tactic. I used it a lot. In the end, it didn't matter. You can get those women out of your head, but it's impossible to get them out of your blood."

Josh was beginning to get that. Oddly, it didn't terrify him half as much as it should have.

It took a great deal of courage for Ashley to call Jo in Boston the minute Josh left. There were things she needed to know. If her life as she knew it was over, she needed to start making an adjustment right now. She'd have to scale down her lifestyle, find a whole new career, maybe even move to some other city.

"Slow down," she scolded herself as she dialed her sister's number. "This isn't the time for making rash decisions. Get the facts first."

Jo picked up on the fourth ring, her tone hesitant.

"Hey, it's me," Ashley said.

"Thank God. I almost didn't pick up."

"Why?"

"The media," Jo said succinctly. "They're trying to track you down. This latest beating—you have heard about it, right?"

"I've heard."

"Well, as you can imagine, it's stirred them up all over again. They want your reaction to it."

"I'm so sorry. You need to get caller ID."

"No, I don't. This will pass. How are you? How did you find out, anyway? I was hoping it hadn't made the news down there."

"There was an item in the Richmond paper," Ashley admitted. "So how bad is it? Are the papers screaming for my head?"

"Of course not," Jo said.

Unfortunately, her baby sister was a terrible liar. Ashley heard the faint hesitation in her voice.

"Come on, Jo. What are they saying? Tell the truth. If you don't, I'll just have to call the office and ask them what's going on. Something tells me they won't sugar-coat anything. I'll be lucky to have a job. They loved having me on board when I was saving the innocent and bringing in great PR for the firm, but now? I can't imagine they're happy about this."

"Okay, it's bad," Jo admitted. "But that's today. The beating just took place yesterday. Everyone's bound to be in an uproar. Things will quiet down in a few days. One paper already put some perspective on the story by asking how the prosecution and cops screwed up the first trial so badly. They've stopped focusing on you completely."

"That doesn't mean I'm off the hook, even with that paper. It just means that the prosecutor and police are dangling on the hook with me," Ashley said cynically. She bit back a sigh. "Maybe I should go back and face the music."

"Absolutely not," Jo said. "You stay right where you are. We're all agreed about that."

"Everyone in the family knows?"

"Mom and Dad do, of course. They've been getting the same calls I have."

"Dammit," Ashley muttered. "I'll call them and tell them not to answer the phone."

"No need. I think Dad's actually enjoying giving the media an earful about irresponsible reporting. You know how he is when anyone picks on one of his baby girls."

The reminder almost brought a smile to Ashley's lips. Max D'Angelo was a stereotypical overly protective Italian father. Nobody hurt one of his daughters.

Heck, it was a wonder any of them had ever had a date, given the way he loomed over every male to cross the threshold. As teenagers, they had all been driven crazy by it.

Now Ashley could only be grateful for her father's innate protectiveness. He'd stand between her and an entire army of reporters and photographers, if need be.

"He's something, isn't he?" she said.

"He loves you to pieces," Jo said. "Don't worry about him and Mom, okay? They just want to be sure you're all right. They think Rose Cottage is the perfect place for you till this mess settles down. They're relieved that you're not here in the thick of it."

"Have you spoken to Maggie or Melanie?"

Jo hesitated. "Don't be furious with me. I did try to call them to let them know what had happened, so they could decide the best way to break the news to you, but neither one was home. This wasn't the kind of message I wanted to leave on a machine. I think you should tell them, though. You shouldn't be alone."

"I'm not alone. Well, I am now, but Josh was here until about a half hour ago. I sent him home."

"Josh?" Jo repeated, immediately intrigued. "Spill, big sister. Who is Josh?"

Ashley was surprised. "You mean the family grapevine has failed you? I thought surely you would have had detailed reports by now. Maggie and Melanie are certainly making a lot out of the fact that I met a man a few hours after my arrival."

"An interesting man?"

"That's one description," she conceded.

"What's a better one?"

Ashley thought about that before answering. "He's soothing," she said eventually.

"Soothing? As in boring?"

She laughed. "No, he's definitely not boring."

"Not the least bit sexy?"

"Oh, he's sexy, all right."

"Really?" Jo said with more enthusiasm. "Now it's getting interesting. Tell me more, Ashley. Are you going to follow the family tradition and fall madly in love while you're at Rose Cottage?"

"Don't be ridiculous. I have way too much on my mind to even think about a man right now."

Jo laughed. "I'm pretty sure love and passion don't require a lot of thinking. You're supposed to go with the flow. Not that I would know, of course, my own love life being what it is."

"Which is?" Ashley asked, eager to steer the subject away from her own problems.

"Not something I care to discuss," Jo said emphatically, in a way that only stirred worry that there was something she was hiding.

Even through her concern, Ashley had to admire her baby sister. No matter how complicated her life got, Jo simply dealt with it. They usually didn't know until much, much later that Jo's emotional life was in turmoil. She was quiet and steady as a rock.

"If you change your mind, I'm here," Ashley said, fully aware that she was wasting her breath.

"I know that. I know I can depend on all of you."

"You just choose not to," Ashley said.

"It's not that I wouldn't value your advice or your support," Jo said. "It just makes it more difficult to know my own mind if there's all this sisterly clamor going on around me."

"Fair enough. I suppose we could listen without offering advice," Ashley offered.

"That'll be the day," Jo said with a laugh. "Maybe one leopard could change its spots, but three? Not a chance."

"Okay, then," Ashley said briskly. "Thanks for filling me in. I'll be in touch."

"If you aren't, I'm coming down there and bringing Mom and Dad with me. We'll circle the wagons."

"Heaven forbid!" Ashley said, truly aghast at the notion.

Jo chuckled. "Thought that would provide sufficient motivation for you to call home more often. Love you."

"You, too, brat."

She hung up the phone slowly and realized she was smiling, despite everything. She might not want her family hovering, but it meant the world to know that they were there if she needed them.

Chapter Seven

Josh arrived at Rose Cottage by 7:00 a.m., but Melanie and Maggie had beaten him there. He spotted their cars as he crossed the backyard from the dock. Something told him that word of Ashley's latest crisis had spread despite his own attempts to keep it under wraps during Mike's visit. He was beginning to realize that the D'Angelo grapevine was an efficient means of communication. He hadn't decided yet if that was good or bad.

He tapped on the back door and walked in to find all three sisters at the kitchen table. Ashley looked as if she were under siege. She turned to him so eagerly, it made his heart skip a beat or two. He wished he could believe that welcome was specifically for him, and wouldn't have been given to anyone who'd walked in the door just then.

"Time to go?" she asked, leaping to her feet. "I'm ready."

"Not so fast, big sister," Maggie said. "Josh, perhaps you would like a cup of coffee before you go?" It wasn't really a question. She was already pouring the coffee, and the determined glint in her eyes was more command than inquiry.

Josh glanced at Ashley and caught the pleading expression in her eyes. Even though he understood and shared her sisters' well-meaning concern, he opted to side with her for now. "Sorry. No time. We have an appointment."

"With some fish," Melanie noted dryly. "I didn't know they kept date books. I imagine they won't be all that disappointed if you're a little late."

"These are very busy fish," Josh retorted, undaunted by her undisguised skepticism. "And you know what they say about early birds."

"They get the worm," Maggie responded. "Which I don't think applies in this instance." She frowned at Ashley, then relented. "Okay, go, but we're not finished with you."

"I think I got that," Ashley said, sounding resigned.

"What time will you be back?" Maggie asked Josh.

"Hard to say," he responded evasively, suspecting they would be waiting on the doorstep if he gave them a specific hour. "With this whole relaxation thing, we try not to think in terms of timetables."

Maggie rolled her eyes. "Oh, please," she scoffed. "I don't know about you, but my sister's brain is equipped with an automatic day planner. I'm relatively certain she has no idea how to turn it off."

"I've noticed," Josh admitted. "We're working on that. She's already made impressive strides. You'd be surprised." He beamed at both of them. "See you."

He stepped aside to let Ashley bolt past him. She was halfway to the dock before he caught up with her. To his shock, she threw her arms around his neck.

"Thank you, thank you, thank you," she enthused. "Your timing was impeccable. I told them you were coming, but they didn't believe me. They thought I was just trying to get rid of them."

He grinned. "Which you were."

"Well, of course."

"I gather someone filled them in about the whole Slocum situation."

"My folks," she admitted. "Had to be, since Jo hadn't been able to reach them. She reluctantly agreed not to call again, but Mom and Dad refused to commit to silence."

"Then you have spoken to your folks since last night?"

"Yes. After I talked to Jo and found out they were being pestered by reporters, I had to call them. I was trying to convince my father to limit himself to 'no comment.'"

Josh heard the combination of frustration and amusement in her voice. "A thankless task?" he guessed.

"You have no idea," she said ruefully. "He's been using this opportunity to vent about media irresponsibility. I suppose I should be grateful. It's doubtful any reporter will call him a second time." She gave him a wistful look. "Can we table this subject till later? Maybe reinstitute the rules of our bet and keep work off-limits? I've done nothing but think about this mess all night long. I could use a break from it."

He noted the dullness in her eyes and the shadows under them.

"Absolutely," he told her. "In fact, once we anchor offshore, you can take a little nap, if you like."

She gave him a surprisingly indignant look. "You're assuming I won't be catching any fish today?"

He chuckled. "You don't even have to cast your line, unless you really want to. Remember, the object is to sort of drift along, watch the clouds roll by and relax. Fishing is just an excuse to leave all your cares behind and be out on the water on a beautiful day."

"I wish I could," she said wistfully.

"You'll get the hang of it," Josh promised. "Sometimes relaxing takes a little effort."

She frowned at him. "Isn't that an oxymoron or something?"

"I suppose it is, if you feel the need to analyze it to death."

She nodded, her expression serious. "Got it. No analyzing. No thinking. Just drifting."

"Exactly."

She settled back against the cushion he'd propped on the seat, tugged down the brim of her cap and closed her eyes. Josh watched as her tensed muscles finally began to relax. Her bare legs and arms were turning a golden brown and her cheeks had a healthy glow, even if it couldn't quite dispel the evidence of her exhaustion. Silently, he waited for her breathing to fall into a slow, steady rhythm.

Just when he thought she'd fallen asleep, she murmured, "Josh?"

"What?"

"Don't you dare catch a fish while I'm taking a break."

"Why not? It's my turn. You've caught all the others."

Her lips quirked in undisguised triumph. "Oh, right, I have, haven't I? I've caught three, and you haven't caught any."

He barely contained a laugh. "And you felt the need to remind me of that because…?"

"Knowing I'm ahead makes it easier to rest."

"Then, by all means, gloat," he replied quietly. "I can take it."

"You're a nice man," she said.

Josh sighed. There it was again. *Nice.* One of these days he was going to have to get around to showing her just how wicked he could be. Something told him that with Ashley in his arms, he could top his very best efforts to date.

The instant Ashley woke up from her nap, she peered into the bucket of salt water. "No fish?" she asked Josh, trying to keep a gloating note out of her voice. It wasn't her fault that she'd turned out to have a knack for it that he seemed to lack.

"Actually I caught five whoppers," he said. "Threw them all back."

"Yeah, right. Speaking of whoppers…"

"Hey, I did," he insisted, his expression perfectly serious. Only the twinkle in his eyes gave him away. "How was your nap?"

"Restful," she admitted.

"Good."

"What time is it? How long did I sleep?"

"A couple of hours, actually. It's almost ten. I was about to slather some more suntan lotion on you."

She grinned. "Sounds like fun," she teased, handing him the bottle. "Just pretend I'm asleep."

"But you're not. You could do it yourself."

"Come on, Josh. Go along with me here. Be daring."

He rolled his eyes. "Okay, sweetheart, you want to take risks, it's fine with me." He took the outstretched bottle, poured lotion in his palm, then told her to turn around.

Ashley jerked when the cool lotion hit her bare shoulders. In a heartbeat, though, she wasn't even aware of the lotion, only of Josh's hands on her skin. It was evident that he had no intention of making quick work of the application. He stroked slowly. He caressed. He sent goose bumps dancing across her flesh until Ashley could hardly breathe.

When his fingers dipped into the low V on her back, skimmed down her spine, then slipped just beneath the fabric of her swimsuit, she almost jumped right out of the boat. He'd turned her taunt into a torment, a seduction. She could feel her nipples beading. Warmth pooled between her thighs. She closed her eyes and sucked in a breath, aware that they were playing a very dangerous game, one he'd apparently anticipated.

"Enough?" Josh asked, his voice suspiciously thick, even though it was evident he was taunting her.

Ashley wasn't quite ready to call it quits. Somehow he'd gotten the upper hand. She wanted it back. "You forgot the front," she told him, slowly turning to face him.

His gaze locked with hers, his eyes glinting wicked sparks. "Do you really, really want me to go on?"

Swallowing hard, she nodded.

He squirted more lotion into his palm, then smoothed it across her chest. His fingers skimmed along the edge of her bathing suit, then took a sudden dip into the cleavage.

"Wouldn't want you to get burned there," he murmured, holding her gaze. "That's very tender skin."

"Uh-huh," she whispered as he shifted his attention to her arms. He seemed to be intent on the soft, pale and surprisingly sensitive underside.

"What about your legs?" he inquired eventually. "Shall I do those?"

Ashley figured she could stand it if he could. "Sure," she said, determined to play out the game she'd started.

Of course, she hadn't realized just how long he could draw out the process. He didn't miss so much as a freckle or a pore, not from the tips of her toes to the tops of her thighs. She was all but coming unglued when he finally pronounced the job done. It took everything in her not to beg him not to stop.

"Thank you," she said primly. "You were very thorough."

"Any job worth doing is worth doing well," he said, a knowing sparkle in his eyes.

She couldn't seem to make herself meet his gaze. "How safe is this water?" she asked.

"For what?"

"Swimming."

"Safe enough. Why?"

Without bothering to respond, she dove over the side of the boat. The water was colder than she'd anticipated, but it felt good against her overheated skin. She finally broke the surface gasping for air, but with her hormones back in check.

"Cool off?" Josh inquired, amusement threading through his voice.

"Sure did," she said cheerfully. "You should try it."

"No, thanks."

"Chicken?"

"You are not going to dare me to dive in there with you," he scolded.

"I just did," she corrected. "I guess you're not up to the challenge."

"Oh, darlin', that was a very bad idea, especially coming from a woman who just washed off most of the suntan lotion she had me put on. Are you angling for another application?"

She saw the worrisome spark of mischief in his eye right before he dove overboard. Just when she was wondering where he was going to surface, he grabbed her ankle and pulled her under. She came up sputtering.

"You rat!" she accused. "That was playing dirty."

"I wasn't aware there were any rules for this particular game," he said, bobbing just beyond her reach. "You gonna get even?"

Her teeth were starting to chatter, but she rose to the bait. "You bet," she said, diving below the surface.

She was so sure he was right in front of her, but the next thing she knew, he'd circled her waist from behind and lifted her out of the water. She shook the hair and water out of her eyes as he slowly turned her around to face him. As her body slid along his, she realized that he was totally and impressively aroused. He fit their bodies together with only the wafer-thin fabric of her swimsuit and his between them, then captured her mouth beneath his. By the time the kiss ended, Ashley was on fire.

She clung to his shoulders and looked into his eyes. "How is it possible to be this hot when the water's like ice?"

"Makes you wonder why there's not steam rising all around us, doesn't it?"

"Oh, yes," she said, not ready to move away from him. Buoyed by the water, she hooked her legs around his waist.

Josh's gaze narrowed. "What are you up to now?"

"Just holding on," she insisted innocently.

"Just tormenting me sounds more like it," he retorted.

She grinned. "Is it working?"

He shifted ever so slightly. "What do you think?"

"Definitely working."

"Are you thinking it's safe to play this kind of game out here because nothing will come of it?" he inquired curiously.

She thought about that. "Yes," she admitted.

"Then you have no intention of going back to dry land and finishing what you've started?"

Taking the question seriously, she gave it some thought. "It's not that I don't want to," she began.

"Same here," he said. "But we've agreed that the timing is all wrong."

She nodded, suddenly feeling guilty. "Sorry. I'm not playing fair, am I?"

"It's not about playing fair," he said. "It's about playing with fire. If you're counting on me being a nice guy and keeping the game under control, don't. Even

I have my limits, Ashley, and you are most definitely testing them."

Ashley heard the somber note in his voice and realized she'd pushed too far. Maybe she'd meant to. Maybe she'd *needed* to, but it wasn't all about her desires. For things to go any further, they really, really needed to be on the same page at the same time.

"How about lunch?" she asked, scrambling back into the boat and pulling a shirt on over her swimsuit. She shivered, despite the warmth of the sun. "I'll buy."

Josh was a little slower getting back in the boat. Once he was seated across from her, he met her gaze, the faint beginnings of a smile tugging at his lips.

"Scary, isn't it?" he asked.

She gave him a puzzled look. "What?"

"Realizing how much you want me."

She couldn't help it. She immediately rose to the challenge. "No more than you want me," she retorted, casting a pointed look at the unmistakable evidence. "But lunch is what's on the agenda, pal."

"Then I think I'll go with a steak sandwich. Something tells me I'm going to need all the stamina I can get as long as you're around."

She shuddered at the promise behind the words. They were going to make love. Perhaps not today, or even tomorrow, but there wasn't a doubt in her mind that neither of them had the willpower to resist the inevitable forever.

By the time they got back to Rose Cottage, Josh was still shaken by the force of his need for Ashley. When she climbed onto the dock, he stayed right where he was.

"You're not coming in?" she asked.

He shook his head. "I'm going home to change. I'll be back to get you in a half hour." After he'd spent twenty minutes of that time in a cold shower. He wasn't hopeful that it would have the desired effect, since a soaking in the icy bay hadn't done a blessed thing to cool off his ardor.

"I'll be waiting," she said, her knowing gaze filled with amusement.

Unfortunately, back at his place there were three messages from Creighton Williams, each sounding more urgent than the one before. Reluctantly, he called the office.

"You need to get back to Richmond this afternoon," his boss said without preamble.

"I'm on vacation," Josh reminded him yet again. It was typical of Creighton to forget, the minute Josh's absence became an inconvenience, that he'd signed off on the vacation request.

"Not anymore," his boss said. "I need you here."

"Why?"

"The judge is moving up the hearing on the Bartholomew acquisition."

"That's your client," Josh reminded him. "Not mine."

"I need you here," his boss insisted. "You know how much Frank Bartholomew respects you. He'll listen to you."

"That's very flattering, but I repeat, he's your client. I'm sure he respects you even more. You've handled his legal matters for years."

Confronted with an indisputable fact, Creighton backed down. "Okay, that's not the only reason I want you back here," he admitted.

"I think you'd better explain, then."

"It'll give you a chance to get together with Stephanie face-to-face and work out this ridiculous argument before it's too late to fix things."

Josh finally saw the ploy for what it really was, a full-court press to get him back together with Stephanie. "Sir, I thought you understood. Stephanie and I didn't have some silly little argument. We're in total agreement that we're not suited to be together. There's nothing between us to fix."

"That's absurd," Creighton barked. "I've given this a lot of thought since we spoke last. This is nothing but premarital jitters. Happens to every man when he sees a wedding date approaching."

"You seem to be forgetting that we never set a wedding date," Josh said. "I'd never even proposed. We only started dating to begin with because it was what you wanted."

"But the inevitability of it was staring you in the face," Creighton said. "Same thing."

"Sir, you don't really need me in court, do you?"

His boss sighed heavily. "No."

"All right, then. I'll be in touch."

"Are you sure you won't reconsider?" Creighton asked, his disappointment evident.

"Absolutely sure, sir. If that's a condition of me coming back, then I'm afraid it's a deal-breaker."

"No, no, I already told you it wasn't," Creighton said impatiently.

"Goodbye, sir." He hung up the phone, glanced at the clock, then called Ashley.

"Where are you? I thought you'd be back by now."

"I had to deal with a crisis. It'll be a few more minutes. Would you rather meet at the café?"

"No, I'll wait. Just hurry. My stomach is rumbling."

When he finally drove up to Rose Cottage, she was already waiting out front.

"You weren't kidding about being starved, were you?" he teased.

"No. Melanie and Maggie ruined my appetite this morning, so I missed breakfast." She regarded him curiously as she slid into the passenger's seat. "Want to tell me about whatever crisis held you up?"

"Later," he said. "It wasn't that important."

"I didn't know there was such a thing as an unimportant crisis."

He laughed. "It depends on which side of the crisis you're on."

"Ah, I'll try to remember that." She glanced out the window. "There's a parking space right there," she pointed out eagerly.

Josh glanced in that direction. "And it's right behind your sister's car, if I'm not mistaken."

Ashley groaned.

"Okay, it's your call. Lunch this second with your sister or drive to someplace else?"

Even before she spoke, Josh figured the audible growling of her stomach pretty much clinched it.

"We'll stay here," she said with undisguised reluctance.

"Don't worry," he soothed. "I'll protect you."

In fact, this could work to his advantage. With Maggie and perhaps even Melanie pestering her, Ashley might forget all about that crisis in his life. He needed to know if he really was going to go back to Richmond and the fast track before he told her that he was a lawyer. He had no idea how she was going to take that news given her own ambivalence about the legal profession these days.

"Oh, look, they're at a table for two," Ashley said happily when she spotted both Maggie and Melanie inside the café. "No room for us."

Of course, no sooner had the words left her mouth than two extra chairs materialized. Apparently Maggie and Melanie had seen them coming and put in a request for the extra seating.

Ashley sighed and dutifully crossed the restaurant.

Maggie studied her with undisguised speculation. "You look amazingly bright-eyed compared to this morning. Was fishing the only thing you all did?"

Josh waited to see how Ashley would field that one. She frowned at her sister.

"That, *little sister,* is none of your business," Ashley said.

"The same way it was none of your business what we did with Mike and Rick?" Melanie inquired sweetly.

Ashley didn't miss a beat. "No. I'm the big sister. I had an obligation to keep an eye on you guys."

"Well, we might be younger, but we're old married ladies now, so it's our obligation to look out for our unmarried big sister."

"In some cultures, you two wouldn't even be married until Ashley here walked down the aisle," Josh reminded them. "You'd be wanting her to hurry up."

Melanie gave him a thoughtful look. "Are you suggesting marriage is already on the table?"

"Good grief, *no,*" Ashley said fervently.

Josh wasn't sure he appreciated the idea being dismissed so readily. "Don't be too hasty," he said, just to rattle her. "It *could* be on the table."

Eyes flashing, she stared him down. "It is *not* on the table," she repeated emphatically.

He grinned. "We'll discuss it later."

"Whose side are you on?" she demanded irritably. "You're just going to get them all stirred up. They won't give us a minute's peace. Mike and Rick will haul you out for some sort of guy talk, which will be only marginally less intimidating than having my father come down here."

Josh shrugged. "They don't scare me."

"Do the words *'What are your intentions?'* scare you?"

Not half as much as he'd expected them to. Not even a tenth as much as they had when Creighton Williams had first uttered them. Obviously, though, they terrified her.

"Settle down, darlin'," he soothed. "Nothing has to be decided till after lunch. You'll be able to think more rationally on a full stomach."

Ashley glowered at him, even as Maggie and Melanie chuckled.

"Go to hell," she muttered, then turned to beckon for the waitress. "I'd like a cheeseburger, fries and a chocolate milk shake."

Her sisters stared at her in shock.

"Oh, my gosh, she really has gone round the bend," Melanie murmured.

Maggie nodded. "Seems that way to me, too."

"I repeat, go to hell," Ashley said, then added, "all of you."

Josh chuckled. "Sounds like her old self to me." And

what a pistol she was. He'd never met anyone like Ashley D'Angelo, and no matter what it took, he was pretty sure it would be a very bad idea to let her get away.

Chapter Eight

If she hadn't been so hungry, Ashley would have gotten up and walked all the way back to Rose Cottage just to get away from Josh and her sisters. They were having entirely too much fun at her expense. As for Josh and those crazy allusions to marriage, he'd apparently stayed underwater too long and killed off a few important brain cells. She wasn't taking him seriously, but her sisters very well might. They were eager to see her follow what they now assumed to be a family tradition and fall wildly in love while staying at Rose Cottage.

Ashley and Josh were on the way home before she called him on his ill-conceived teasing. "What on earth were you thinking?" she asked testily.

"About?"

"Oh, don't pretend you don't know exactly what I'm

talking about," she retorted. "I'm referring to all that nonsense about marriage."

He gave her a look filled with feigned innocence. "Maybe it wasn't nonsense."

"If it wasn't, then you're the one who needs his head examined. I know absolutely nothing about the state of your life beyond the fact that you just broke up with some other woman, but I think we can agree that the turmoil in mine is sufficient to preclude any serious talk of the future."

"There's no harm in getting the idea out there, though, is there?"

She gave him an impatient look. "My professional life is in chaos. Don't you think I have enough to worry about without pondering marriage to a man I barely know?"

"I don't know. Thinking about getting married could be more fun than thinking about torts and trials and things over which you have no control, such as public opinion." He glanced over at her. "Don't you agree?"

The man was totally exasperating. "Marriage is not some game, dammit! You start tossing that word around with my family, and you'll be in front of a minister before you can catch your breath. Haven't you noticed that my sisters both married after whirlwind courtships? They think it's a family tradition, and they think it's all tied up with staying in Rose Cottage, as if the place had some sort of magical powers in the love department."

He grinned. "It's a unique tradition, all right. As for the cottage being enchanted, didn't you ever see that old movie?"

She sighed heavily. "Yes, I saw it. It doesn't apply. Don't you take anything seriously?"

"Sure. Actually I take marriage very seriously. That's why I broke things off with that other woman. I realized I wasn't serious enough about her for marriage. We were wasting time together in a relationship that was going nowhere. She deserved better than that."

"Then why are you joking around about the whole marriage thing with me?"

Now he sighed. "I'm not entirely sure," he admitted eventually. "The words just seemed to pop out. Since no panic alarms have gone off, I've seen no reason to take them back. Besides, it's given your sisters something to chew on besides your career status. It's pretty much gotten *your* attention off that, too."

She regarded him doubtfully. "So this has been some sort of magnanimous gesture on your part to get my sisters off my case?"

"Something like that," he said, then winked. "For now, anyway."

She studied him helplessly. "I don't know what to make of you."

"Ditto, darlin', but aren't we going to have fun figuring things out?"

That was precisely the problem, Ashley thought a little desperately. She *was* having fun, perhaps too much fun given the fact that she had an army of reporters on her trail, a career in turmoil and a guilty conscience over her part in freeing a confessed murderer.

Determined to get things back on a far safer track, she regarded Josh seriously. "What are your plans this afternoon?"

"Kicking back. Nothing much."

"Good. Then you can help me make a list."

He regarded her warily. "What kind of list?"

"Career decisions," she said with grim determination. "I could use an outside perspective."

"Bad idea," he said.

"It has to be done," she insisted. "Maybe you have all the time in the world to relax, but I can't sit around wallowing in indecisiveness indefinitely."

He chuckled. "How many days have you been wallowing in anything here?"

"Three, four, something like that." To her amazement, she couldn't remember precisely. Maybe she was getting too good at the whole relaxation thing. That should be a warning to her. She needed to get focused—fast. A life without focus was a life that could spin out of control. Of course, hers had managed to slip off the track even with all her safeguards in place....

"And you're going to be here three weeks," Josh said. "Isn't that what you told me the night we met?"

She nodded. "What's your point?"

"You're pushing for too much, too fast. The real answers won't come to you for at least another week or so."

"Why on earth would you say a thing like that?"

"It's a proven fact that you have to spend serious time unwinding before you can get in touch with your real heart's desire."

"A proven fact?" she echoed skeptically.

He nodded. "Absolutely. Trying to force things will just set you back. You'll wind up with a decision that's based on logic, not emotion."

"You are so full of it, Madison."

"But I'm charming," he said with the engaging smile that never failed to make her heart take a tumble in her chest. "And you have to admit that the whole relaxation thing is working out exactly as I predicted."

"True," she admitted reluctantly. "But what's wrong with logic? The world would be a better place if everyone made their decisions based on logic."

He shook his head. "No. It's critical to factor emotion into the equation. Without it, we'd all be dutiful little drones. Trust me on this. You can't be making lists this soon, or you'll just have a bunch of cut-and-dried choices."

She sighed heavily. "Then what on earth will I do with the rest of the afternoon?"

"I have a plan," he said cheerfully.

"Why doesn't that surprise me?"

"Actually, it was your sister's idea."

She regarded him suspiciously. "Which one?" She was pretty sure any ideas tossed out by Melanie would involve getting all those tulip and daffodil bulbs in the ground.

"Maggie. Why? What difference does it make?"

"Never mind. What sort of brainstorm did she share with you?"

"Trust me, it'll be fun."

She was about to protest that she wasn't going anywhere with him without details, but then she fell silent. The truth was, she *did* trust him, even though she knew precious little about him beyond his name and his ability to bait a hook. Given the way she was feeling about the whole trust thing these days, that was nothing short of a miracle.

She glanced at him and saw that he was grinning as he awaited her decision. "Okay, you win," she said.

"See, now, putting yourself into my hands wasn't so hard, was it?" he teased.

She uttered a self-mocking laugh. "Actually, you have no idea how hard it was."

But something told her it was a huge step in the right direction.

When Josh turned into the driveway at Maggie's, he saw Ashley stiffen beside him.

"We're going to my sister's? Why? So she can cross-examine us some more? That sounds like fun."

"The trust business doesn't run very deep with you, Ashley, does it?" he asked, amused.

"Frankly, no."

"Well, cool your jets, lady lawyer. We're not here to visit. In fact, as far as I know, Maggie's not even home."

"Then why are we here?"

"It's an orchard," he reminded her with exaggerated patience. "We're going to pick apples."

She stared at him blankly. "Why?"

"Because it's something you've never done before. Neither have I. We can share the experience. People bond over new experiences."

"And I suppose we'll bond even more as we share a hospital room when we both wind up with broken arms," she said cheerfully.

"You're not approaching this with the right attitude," he scolded. "We're young. We're limber. How hard can it be?"

"Unless you think you're going to shake the tree and have apples fall into our baskets, it's going to be work, Madison." Her expression brightened. "Watching you get the hang of it could be amusing, though."

Josh parked the car at the edge of the orchard. "You

can forget that idea. This is a joint venture. And Maggie has promised to bake us an apple pie when we're done."

"An apple pie, huh? That can't take more than a couple of apples, right? Okay, I can do that."

Josh gave her a chiding look. "It'll take more than a couple for the pie, then we'll want some apples for our picnic tomorrow and some for snacks later on. Plus we haven't even decided which kind we want. I like Granny Smith. How about you?"

"I should have known you'd prefer something tart. I like the sweet ones. I'm not sure we have a choice, though. I think all these trees are Golden Delicious."

"Not according to Maggie."

"When did you two have this heart-to-heart about apples?"

"When I was here the other night."

"So you've been planning this outing since then?"

"No, I've been planning this since lunchtime, when I recalled the conversation she and I had after dinner. In relaxation mode, it's not acceptable to plan too far ahead."

"Which is why the whole marriage thing is so absurd," she said. "If that's not planning way ahead, I don't know what is."

"A valid point," he admitted. "We'll table that for this afternoon, though I find it interesting that you haven't forgotten it for a second." He glanced up at the trees that were laden with fruit, all out of reach. "I think getting to those apples is going to require all of our concentration."

He met her gaze. "Ever climb a tree before?"

"Do I look as if tree-climbing were a hobby of mine?"

"You could have been a tomboy. How am I supposed to know?" At least one of the D'Angelo sisters had been. He could recall their grandmother lamenting it to his mother. Neither Melanie or Maggie seemed the tree-climbing type, so maybe it had been Jo, the one he hadn't met yet.

"Trust me, not a tomboy," she said.

He gave her a very thorough once-over. "Just as well. I would hate to think of that smooth skin all scraped and scarred." Then again, he could have had himself a grand time kissing any imperfections. He decided not to share that intriguing thought.

"If that's the case, why would you insist on sending me up into a tree to pick apples now?" she inquired.

"Because we're old enough and wise enough now not to take unnecessary chances."

"Ha! I've seen glimpses of your daredevil side."

He climbed out of the car. "Come on, Ashley, stop whining. This is going to be fun." He looked around. "There should be a ladder out here somewhere, and some baskets."

"Let me know when you find them," she called out, still tucked into place in the car.

"You are not getting into the spirit of this," he accused.

"What was your first clue?"

He walked over to the car and rested his elbows on the passenger windowsill, then looked deep into her eyes. "Do you really, really hate this whole idea? We can do something else."

Suddenly a grin spread across her face. "Nope. Just seeing how far I could push you before you let me have my way. Bring on the ladder, Madison. If you want to pick your own apples for a pie, then I'm right there with you. Never let it be said that I'm not up for a challenge."

"In the tree?" he inquired, just to be sure he understood the degree of her capitulation.

"At the very tip-top," she confirmed.

He didn't like the worrisome glint in her eyes. "Don't get carried away."

"Hey, once you've gotten my enthusiasm all stirred up, it's too late to try to rein me in." She scrambled from the car. "I see the ladder. Last one in the tree turns into a toad."

Josh didn't even try to catch up with her. He had a hunch the view from the ground while she tore up that ladder was going to be something. He strolled over, steadied the ladder and took a long, leisurely survey of her trim backside and endless bare legs as she climbed agilely to the top.

"You lose," she called down, sounding triumphant.

"No way, darlin'. You may be at the top of that tree, but I am definitely the big winner here."

She scowled down from her precarious perch on a branch high above him. "How do you figure that?"

"I've got the better view."

It took a minute for her to realize what he meant. She immediately pelted him with an apple. The damn thing hit him right in the head.

"Hey, that hurt," he protested, laughing as he dodged another one.

"That was the idea. Didn't you ever play baseball? Maybe you should learn to catch. Otherwise, all we'll have is applesauce."

Josh heard the branch creak suspiciously before Ashley realized she was in danger. "Ashley, don't move," he said urgently.

Naturally she twisted around just to annoy him. The creak became a sharp crack, and suddenly she was falling. He had a split second to position himself to catch her. They both landed on the ground, but at least he'd managed to cushion her fall. The impact knocked the wind out of him.

As soon as he could speak, his gaze locked on hers. "You okay?"

"Uh-huh," she murmured, looking dazed.

"You don't sound okay. How many fingers am I holding up?"

She gave him an impatient look. "Two. I didn't hit my head, Josh. I landed on my butt, on top of you, as a matter of fact. Maybe you're the one we should be worrying about. Can you move?"

He grinned at her. "Why would I want to? I have a beautiful woman sprawled across me."

She immediately went still. "So I am. Maybe I should take advantage of that."

Now she was the one making him nervous. "How?"

She framed his face in her hands and kissed him. It was the kind of impulsive, no-holds-barred kiss that had taken them to the edge of a meltdown before. Just because they were in the middle of her sister's orchard didn't mean he had the sense to turn down what she was offering. He kissed her back. It didn't seem to matter that the ground was cold and hard or that a cloud had passed over the sun. The only things that mattered were the soft curves that fit his body like the other half of a puzzle and the intoxicating scent of her perfume.

His hands cupped her butt and held her more tightly in place. It took everything in him not to start to move, not to begin the motions that would carry them past the point of no return. He was hard and aching. She was making little purring noises deep in her throat, the kind of sounds of pure pleasure and need that could drive a man wild.

Her mouth was greedy on his, her movements restless. Another five seconds and he was going to lose the fragile grip he had on his control. Only the grim determination not to have their first time together be on the ground not two hundred yards from her sister's house kept him from granting her what she obviously wanted.

"Slow down, darlin'," he said. "You don't want this."

"Yes, I do," she insisted.

"Not here, I suspect. We're in your sister's orchard," he reminded her, then grinned as her eyes snapped open and she looked around.

"Oh, my God," she said, scrambling away from him. "What was I thinking?"

"Thinking had nothing to do with it. One of these days we need to find a nice, comfortable bed and try this again. I think we can eliminate the bay and the orchard as being bad ideas." He grinned at her. "Should we hunt one down now?"

She scrubbed a hand across her face, like a child trying to wake up from a dream. "No." She regarded him helplessly. "I was going to be so sensible about this. I was going to permit myself to have a wild, passionate fling with you."

He heard the past tense and felt his stomach clench. "And now?"

"Now it's gotten complicated." She met his gaze. "Hasn't it?"

"It's only as complicated as we let it be."

"What kind of guy response is that? It's either complicated or it isn't."

He knew better than to laugh at her obvious frustration. "Allow me to clarify. Sex is uncomplicated. Making love gets a bit trickier. Where are you coming from?"

Her gaze met his, then darted away, before finally returning. "I honestly don't know anymore. Do you?"

"Can't say that I do, but there's no rush to figure it out," he reminded her.

"Do you back-burner everything in your life until it's convenient?" she asked.

He thought of the demanding schedule he maintained at work and nearly laughed. Since he didn't want to go there, he restrained himself. "Would you believe me if I said no?"

"How could I? You seem to me to epitomize the concept of putting everything off till tomorrow."

"And you never put anything off," he commented. "Maybe I'm just trying to lead you to a middle ground. The truth is, we tend to make our own chaos. Sure, the real world has deadlines and they're important, but we turn everything into a must-do crisis. Not everything needs to be done immediately. We can take the pressure off ourselves. We can choose not to participate in the rat race. All it takes is recognizing our own limits, prioritizing and learning to say no."

Putting that into words for her finally gave him the sense of direction he'd been craving for himself. It was just as he'd tried to tell her—answers came as soon as a person stopped trying to force them.

"If you don't grab at opportunities when they present themselves, how do you get ahead?" Ashley asked, obviously perplexed.

"Why do you have to?" he countered. "What's wrong with just loving what you do and setting a pace that allows you to live your life? Isn't that exactly what you're wrestling with while you're here? Isn't it the truth that you've allowed work to consume you to the point that the situation you find yourself in now leaves you with the sick feeling that your life as you've known it is over?"

A smile tugged at her lips. "That's exactly how I would feel if you didn't keep distracting me. As it is, the only thing I seem to be wrestling with is you."

"Is that such a bad thing?"

She held his gaze for what seemed an eternity, then finally shook her head. "No, as a matter of fact, it's not bad at all."

Josh nodded in satisfaction. It seemed both of them were finding unexpected answers this afternoon.

Chapter Nine

For once the thing that kept Ashley awake all night was the restless anticipation Josh stirred in her, rather than all the uncertainty about her professional future. A part of her wished they'd just gotten their first time over with, so the edginess would be a thing of the past. Instead, she was lying in bed remembering the way his body felt next to hers, the way he tasted and smelled, the way his skin heated when she touched him.

"Oh, please," she moaned when the image grew so steamy she was ready to scream in frustration. If she didn't have at least one lingering ounce of pride, she would crawl out of her bed right this instant, drive to his place and crawl into his. She doubted he would turn her away.

Still, it was a point of honor to wait for the right timing, whatever the heck that was. Josh seemed to have some vague idea that they would recognize it when it happened. She wasn't so sure. She just thought it was going to get increasingly frustrating until one or both of them exploded and they had sex on some tabletop in plain view of half the world. The idea didn't seem nearly as appalling as it should. That's how desperate Ashley was feeling.

What puzzled her was that it was a man like Josh, as laid-back as any human being she'd ever known, who stirred such passionate feelings in her. If he had even the tiniest streak of ambition in him, she'd never seen a glimpse of it. Heck, he was so low-key about work, she still didn't know exactly what he did. Whatever it was couldn't be too demanding, since he seemed to have an endless amount of time for their lazy fishing trips. She gathered he was on vacation at the moment, but he seemed so at ease, she couldn't imagine he had a high-pressure career.

Not that there was a thing in the world wrong with being content in some noncareer-track job with few demands and an obviously lax timetable, but it was totally alien to the world she'd been living in since graduating from law school. She couldn't imagine being with a man who had such low aspirations.

But, truthfully, she could imagine being with Josh. She found him to be oddly soothing, yet stimulating, which turned out to be an intriguing and unexpected combination.

She was still tossing and turning as she considered all that when the phone rang at dawn. She fumbled for the receiver. "Yes?"

"Ashley, it's Jo."

There was an unmistakably somber note in her youngest sister's voice that had Ashley sitting upright and fully alert in a heartbeat. "What's wrong?"

"I just tuned in to the morning news. They had an interview with your boss."

Ashley's heart began to thud dully. "And? Did he throw me to the wolves?"

"No. Actually he said a lot of nice things about you, but I don't think you're going to be happy about it. He's acting as if what happened in court is no big deal," Jo said indignantly. "He says all defense lawyers assume their clients are guilty. He says you were just doing your job and doing it exceedingly well, that he's proud of you."

Ashley knew she should have felt vindicated by Wyatt Blake's defense of her actions, but the unwarranted praise sickened her. It was as if he were finding a way to capitalize on what had happened in court. Obviously the PR consultant the firm kept on retainer had shown him a way to spin the story that would work to the firm's benefit. She hated that he was using the lowest moment of her career to get publicity for the firm.

"And you know the worst thing?" Jo asked. "He acted as if your feeling bad about getting Tiny off was naive. He said it in that patronizing tone of his. You know the one, Ashley. I've always found it offensive and wondered how you put up with it. Hearing it directed at *you* made me want to throw something at the TV."

Ashley had been expecting Wyatt Blake to make a public comment sooner or later, but not like this. Her respect for the man who'd once been her mentor diminished to zero. On some level she'd expected it to come to this. She really wasn't as naive as her boss had implied, but she hadn't been prepared for the awful taste it left in her mouth.

"I need to come home," Ashley said. "It's time for me to speak out. And I need to see Wyatt and let him know I don't appreciate his misguided attempt to turn this into some sort of legal triumph." If she left in the next half hour, she could be there by nightfall, in plenty of time to confront Wyatt in his office.

"No," Jo said fiercely. "You can't come home yet. You'll just make things worse."

"I'm sorry, but I don't see how they could get much worse."

"You're angry. You're liable to lash out and wind up behind bars yourself."

"I lash out with words. Not even the powerful Wyatt Blake can have me locked up for that."

"Still, he can make it very unpleasant for you if you try to contradict the spin he's putting out there," Jo said reasonably. "I didn't call to get you so riled up you'd come home. I called to warn you, so you could start thinking about whether you want to work for a firm that would twist things like this just for the chance to get some free publicity."

Ashley already knew in her heart that she could never go back there. In fact, even without a plan, she was tempted to call and quit right now, but she wouldn't. Actions taken in haste were too often regretted. Her sister was right about that.

She wouldn't go back to Boston, either. She'd stay here, think things through logically and then when she was confident that she was making a sound decision, she'd go home.

Then she'd rip the man's heart out for lumping her in with all the other criminal defense lawyers who didn't give a rip about their clients' innocence or guilt as long as the bills were paid and the headlines were big enough.

"Thanks for calling, Jo. I promise I won't do anything rash."

"You know that none of this changes anything about how the rest of us feel about you, right? We're still proud of you," Jo said. "We're behind you a thousand percent."

Tears immediately stung Ashley's eyes. "I don't deserve you."

"Of course you do," Jo said impatiently. "You're the first one there when one of us is in trouble. How could we do any less for you? Now do something fun today and forget all about that sleazeball Blake. He's not worth one second of your time."

"I'll try," she promised, though she knew it would be impossible. How could she forget that yet another man she'd trusted and respected had betrayed her? She knew he'd insist that it was all a necessary PR move for the firm, and maybe he was even right about that, but it still felt lousy being used in such a despicable way.

Even though she'd promised Jo that she wouldn't do anything hasty, even though she'd told herself it was a bad idea, she punched in Wyatt Blake's number and waited for him to pick up his private line.

"Blake here," he said, sounding distracted, probably from fielding so many media requests at the crack of dawn.

"Couldn't wait to capitalize on the furor over the Slocum acquittal, could you, Wyatt?"

"Ashley, where on earth are you?" he asked, not

sounding particularly guilt-stricken to hear her voice. "I tried to catch up with you to get you back here. We had to get a statement on the record. Ever since Slocum got off, we've been inundated with calls from the media. We had to get our position out there. We didn't have a choice. This thing's turned into a goldmine in terms of publicity. You could be in front of the cameras every night on the evening news."

Listening to him recite the line he'd obviously been given by the very powerful public relations firm they kept on retainer, she knew what she had to do. If he didn't think he had a choice, then neither did she.

"I'll give you a whole new spin, Wyatt. In your next press release, you can announce that I've quit. That ought to give the firm a few more of those headlines you so obviously covet."

"Quit? You can't do that," he said, unmistakable panic in his voice. "Come on, Ashley, think about this. You can name your own price these days."

They both knew the panic stemmed from his awareness that she pulled in the firm's highest number of billable hours each month. The media attention she drew was another plus. The partners wouldn't be happy to see all of that disappear.

"I can't work with people who obviously don't appreciate the value I put on my reputation or who deliberately diminish the fact that I have a conscience. We agreed when I came there that I wouldn't take just any case, that I wouldn't be a pawn for some rich guy who's guilty as sin, but needs a great defense."

"And we've let you do that, haven't we?"

"Yes, but in one press conference you pretty much

shattered whatever faith the public might have had that I was an honest, straight-shooting lawyer."

"Tiny Slocum did that," Wyatt said, his tone suddenly hard and unyielding. "I was just trying to make the best of it."

Ashley could see his point. She just couldn't live with it.

"Face it, Wyatt, I'm no good to you anymore," she said.

"Ashley, I'm sorry as hell you see it that way. I brought you into this company. No one's been prouder of your work than I've been."

"But you obviously never really knew or respected me. It only took you a few hours to turn me into a hero for something you know I'm ashamed about," she reminded him. "I might have made a terrible mistake when I believed in my client, but you've made an even bigger one. You thought I'd be so low, I'd let you use me and be thrilled about it. It's not going to be that way. I'll have someone come by to clear out my office."

She hung up before he could say another word. Oddly, rather than sheer gut-wrenching terror, all she felt was relief. It was the first time in days that she knew with absolute clarity that she'd done the right thing.

As for what came next, she was going to take a page out of Josh's book and wait and see. She had money in the bank, a roof over her head and people who loved her. Maybe it was time she counted her blessings, the ones that really mattered.

Josh was sound asleep when his phone rang. He rolled over and fumbled for it, then mumbled a greeting.

"Wake up, Madison. Something tells me the fish are

going to be biting again today," Ashley said, sounding more cheerful than she had in days.

Josh sat up and rubbed his eyes. Funny thing how just the sound of her voice could snap him wide awake. In an instant he was alert enough to hear the edge of hysteria behind all that cheeriness. "What's happened?"

"I'll tell you when I see you. Hurry up. I'll have the coffee on when you get here."

The promise of coffee had him rolling out of bed and reaching for his pants. Okay, maybe it wasn't just the thought of caffeine. Maybe it was Ashley's odd mood. He was curious about what could have happened since he'd left her the night before. Despite that bright tone of hers, he had a feeling it wasn't anything good.

There was a distinct chill in the air when he went outside. Fall had evidently arrived during the night. He went back for a sweater and jeans to wear over his swimsuit and T-shirt.

It was even colder on the water, but by the time he'd rowed to Rose Cottage and tied the boat up to the dock, he was warm.

Ashley was waiting for him at the back door, a cup of coffee in hand. "Thought you might need this right away. You didn't sound too alert on the phone."

"I'd decided to sleep in," he said, giving her a peck on the cheek and studying her curiously, looking for evidence of turmoil in her eyes. Her expression was perfectly bland.

"Why were you sleeping in?"

"Because I could."

She laughed. "And I picked today to call at the crack of dawn. Sorry," she said without much real evidence of regret.

"No problem. What's up with you? You seem awfully cheerful this morning."

She lifted her cup of coffee in a mock toast. "I am, actually. I quit my job."

Josh blinked hard, sure he had to have heard wrong. A workaholic who'd just quit usually wasn't quite so chipper. At least that explained the barely concealed note of hysteria he thought he'd detected in her voice earlier.

"When did you do that?"

"About an hour ago."

"I thought you were going to take my advice and let things mull a while longer before making any decisions about the future."

She shrugged. "Things change."

"Such as?"

"My hand was forced," she said succinctly. "I did what I had to do."

"And you're okay with that?"

"I'm sure the sheer terror will set in eventually, but yes, at the moment, I am ecstatic. I am feeling strong and in control."

"I see. Mind telling me why you woke up at dawn and decided that the first thing you'd do this morning was to turn in your resignation?"

She gave him an apparently condensed version of what her sister had told her and her subsequent conversation with the senior partner in her law firm.

"How could I go on working for people like that?" she asked.

"You couldn't," Josh agreed without hesitation. He would have done the same thing. "I'm just surprised you didn't wait till you had something else lined up."

She shrugged. "So am I, but it seemed like the right thing to do at the time, so I went with the flow."

His gaze narrowed. "You aren't going to blame this on *me* later, are you?"

"How could I? You weren't even here."

"But the whole go-with-the-flow philosophy," he reminded her. "I've been its biggest proponent around here."

"And an excellent philosophy it is," she said happily. "Trust me, it won't come back to bite you in the butt, not even if I wind up destitute."

"Good to know. Have you given any thought to what happens next?"

"No. I'm on vacation."

"Actually, you're out of work. It's not exactly the same thing," he said, though he had to admire her new attitude. She seemed to be embracing it with surprising enthusiasm. Unfortunately, he wasn't buying the act for a minute.

She waved off his reminder. "Not going to worry about it today. Let's go fishing."

He nodded slowly. "Fishing it is."

"I packed a lunch. I thought we could stay out a really long time."

"Okay," he said slowly. "Why?"

"Because once my family gets wind of this, they're going to think I've lost my mind. I don't do impulsive things. I don't do much of anything except work. I'd rather not be around when they show up with a shrink."

He laughed. "You may surprise them, but I doubt they'd go that far."

She held out an obviously heavy picnic hamper and a cooler, then said grimly, "I'm not taking any chances."

* * *

Ashley really appreciated Josh's silence. Either he was in shock or he was showing amazing restraint. Whichever it was, at least he wasn't pestering her with questions for which she had no answers.

They'd been out on the water for a couple of hours. He'd caught several fish that he declared to be too small. He'd tossed them back. Ashley hadn't even felt a faint stirring of her usual competitive spirit, which suggested she was more shaken by the morning's events than she'd realized.

"Josh?"

"Hmm?"

She nudged his foot. "Wake up."

"I am awake."

"Then look at me."

He tilted his sunglasses down and peered at her over the top. "Yes?"

"Do you think I made a terrible mistake? Be honest."

"Doesn't matter what I think. Do you?"

"No."

"Then there's your answer."

"Do you think any other firm in Boston will touch me after this?"

He appeared to give the question careful consideration. "That's hard to say," he replied eventually. "You're a good lawyer with a fantastic track record. I'd think that once the publicity dies down, any firm would be happy to take you on." He met her gaze. "Or you could start your own firm and capitalize on the notoriety."

She shuddered at that idea. How could she take advantage of all the negative publicity, when that was exactly what she'd accused Wyatt of doing? It seemed sleazy and opportunistic. "Are you serious?"

"It's just an option. I'm not making recommendations here, just tossing out ideas."

"Any others?"

"You could always open a firm here," he suggested.

His expression was casual, but she had the distinct impression that he'd given this particular option a lot of thought long before this morning's turn of events. "Here? There are probably plenty of lawyers here now."

"One or two," he said, almost sounding as if he'd looked into it. "The area's growing. You might not get rich, but you'd do okay."

Stay here in the boondocks? The idea held more appeal than it might have when she'd first arrived, intending to endure her three-week banishment from Boston, but to stay forever? Wouldn't she go nuts after a few months? A year at the outside? How challenging could the cases be? She'd be defending the occasional DUI charge or maybe a drug dealer. Those were not the kind of crimes on which she'd built her reputation. She'd handled the high-profile white-collar crime, the occasional sensational murder case. She would miss that.

Or would she? Having seen the dark side of that kind of law, was it still what she wanted? She honestly didn't know. She wasn't quite ready to turn her back on it, at least not without exploring all of her options.

"Maybe I could go to D.C.," she suggested instead. "Or even Richmond."

"You could," he agreed, though he looked oddly disappointed by her response.

She studied him intently. "Josh, is there some reason

you want me to stay here? Say, for the sake of speculation, that I did, are you thinking that we'd go on being together? Is that your agenda?"

He grinned at her careful phrasing. "The thought did cross my mind. It might give us time to find that suitable bed we keep talking about."

It would also change the dynamics of everything. If she was leaving, she was free to indulge in a wildly passionate fling. If she was staying, then she'd be toying with a relationship. She didn't think she'd be any good at that.

"I don't know," she said honestly. "I can't base a decision about my entire professional future on what might or might not happen with the two of us."

"I'm not asking you to. I'm just giving you something to consider while you're weighing all those options."

"I need to make a list," she said, frustrated by the magnitude of the decisions facing her. She'd known all along that it would eventually come to this, but she'd avoided confronting it. Now she had to. No matter what Josh said to the contrary, proper decision-making required organization, not drifting around in a rowboat.

"Not today," he chided. "The list is already dancing around in your head. It will sort itself out if you give it enough time."

"This is my life. I can't just wait around for the stars to align or something," she said impatiently. She could only do the go-with-the-flow thing for so long. As of seven o'clock this morning when she'd quit her job, it had outlived its usefulness.

He laughed. "Come here," he urged.

She studied him suspiciously. "Why?"

"Just wriggle your sexy bottom over here next to me. Otherwise, I'll just have to come over there."

Filled with suspicion, she finally maneuvered until she was next to him. He put his arm around her.

"Rest your head right here," he said, patting his shoulder.

After a moment's hesitation, she leaned against his chest, tucked her head on his shoulder and heaved a sigh.

"That's better," he said. "Now close your eyes."

"Why?"

"Because I said to."

She bristled at that. "You're not—"

"I know," he said with amusement, cutting off her protest. "I am not the boss of you."

"Right."

"Just trust me. Close your eyes."

She finally permitted her eyelids to drift shut.

"Clear your head," he instructed. "Just concentrate on the sound of the water lapping against the boat, and on the sun on your face. Let everything else go."

Out of sheer habit and stubbornness, she fought it, but eventually his soothing tone relaxed her and her mind finally slipped away to a calmer, more tranquil place.

"This isn't so bad, is it?" he asked eventually, his voice low.

"What?" she murmured.

"Being here, with me, just existing in the moment."

She smiled. "No," she admitted, filled with wonder at just how right it felt. "It's not bad at all."

"Then why would you give it up one second before you have to?" he asked.

Good question, she thought, right before she snuggled more tightly against him. Why give up something that felt this right? She'd eventually have to think about that, worry it to death, in all probability, but not right now. In fact, it could wait till later.

She sighed happily. Much, much later.

Chapter Ten

To Ashley's dismay, the entire D'Angelo family was waiting at Rose Cottage when she and Josh got back late in the afternoon. She scowled at Jo. "Your doing?"

"Don't blame your sister," her mother said, stepping forward to give her a fierce hug. "Your father and I decided it was time to come down here and give you some moral support. We booked a flight right after that awful morning newscast today. Jo tried to talk us out of it, but when we insisted, she refused to be left behind."

She leaned back and searched Ashley's face. "How are you holding up?"

To Ashley's total chagrin, the sympathetic note in her mother's voice was the last straw. She burst into tears. To her shock—and probably everyone else's—it was Josh who stepped forward and tucked a finger under her chin.

"Want to go for a walk?" he asked solemnly. "Get your bearings?"

She looked into his eyes and felt the ground steady under her feet. What an amazing thing, that a man she'd known only a few days could have that effect on her. She'd have to explore the reasons for that later, when her entire family wasn't standing around smirking. Her mother might be a bit perplexed by Josh's presence, but if they hadn't done so before, her sisters were probably now planning her wedding to the man.

Her father stepped up just then, and with a scowl in Josh's direction, took his place. "You sure you're okay, kitten?"

Hearing her childhood nickname that only her father had ever dared to call her almost brought on another round of tears, but she managed to blink them away and offer him a beaming smile.

"I'm fine," she assured him, giving his hand a squeeze. Then she announced brightly, "Since everyone's here and probably starved, let's go out for crabs." She linked an arm through her mother's, hoping to wipe the worried frown off her face. "Remember Grandma's favorite place? It was always our very first stop when we came in the summer."

Her mother dutifully fell in with the obvious distraction, and for once her sisters even cooperated. Ashley glanced back at Josh and mouthed, "Thank you."

He grinned. "Not a problem." He turned and headed toward the water.

Ashley stopped in her tracks and stared after him. "Hey, Madison, where do you think you're going?"

"Home," he said.

"I don't think so." She sent the others on ahead and went back for him. "I need you there. Please don't bail on me now."

"Why not? You've got an entire family to lean on tonight."

"Which is precisely why I want you there, to protect me from their overly zealous questions."

"Don't you think my presence during this crisis will create a few questions, as well?"

She stood on tiptoe and kissed him. "In case you missed it, they already have questions. A lot of them, if I'm not mistaken. Not to worry, though. We can handle them."

He looked doubtful. "Think so?"

"I know so."

"Did you see the way your father was looking at me? If I hadn't moved aside, I think he would have taken a punch at me."

Ashley laughed. "He looks at any male who's ever come within a mile of any of us exactly the same way. It didn't scare off Mike or Rick. And I promise you, Dad's all bluster. He's never slugged anyone as far as I know."

"All right, then," he said. "Anything those two can do, I can do."

"That's the spirit." She met his gaze. "One last thing before we join the others. Have I mentioned how grateful I am that you were here for me today?"

"My pleasure."

It was a rare man who didn't mind having a woman dump all her problems and insecurities in his lap. She studied him curiously. "One of these days we're going to have to talk about you for a change. Somehow, from the moment we met, it's all been about me."

He laughed. "Also my pleasure. You're much more fascinating than I am."

"I don't believe that. I think there are hidden depths to Josh Madison I should be exploring."

To her surprise, her teasing remark was met with an unexpected wariness.

"My life's an open book," he said, though his declaration lacked conviction.

"Then it's past time I started reading it," she said. "I've been totally self-absorbed, and you've graciously let me get away with it. I promise that's going to change." Even if it meant that her feelings for him grew even stronger and more complicated than they were now.

That flicker of wariness appeared once more in his eyes, as if he viewed her words not as a well-meant promise but as a threat.

What was it that Josh didn't want her to find out? Up until five minutes ago, Ashley would have sworn that he truly was an open book and that she knew everything important there was to know about him. She knew he had character and strength and compassion. She'd been so sure that was everything that really mattered. Now she wasn't certain of that at all.

It was time to fish or cut bait, Josh concluded as he sat with the D'Angelos at dinner. He let the conversation swirl around him, all of it lively and filled with the laughter he'd once imagined enviously from his own lonely house down the road. He could put Ashley off for a few more hours or possibly even a few more days as long as her folks stuck around, but he'd seen that glint of determination in her eyes. She wasn't going to be put off indefinitely.

How was she going to react when she discovered that he, too, was a lawyer, especially one who was about to make a decision to get out of the rat race and settle into a quiet country practice? Given the way she'd reacted when he'd floated a similar plan for her own career, he suspected she wasn't going to be impressed.

It was funny, though, that talking to her about it had just about solidified his own resolve. Whatever happened between them, he was going to settle here. He'd rediscovered the rare contentment he hadn't known since childhood, and he wanted it back on a permanent basis. Before he made the decision final, though, he needed to be absolutely sure that his contentment wasn't due entirely to Ashley's intriguing presence, that it wouldn't vanish if she did.

There would be other differences, too. He doubted he'd be able to fish all morning long, at least not if he expected to earn a living, but he imagined he could get out on the water for an hour or so most days. And this was a great place to raise a family. He'd been thinking about that more and more as he'd envisioned a future with Ashley. Her sisters had seen it. Why couldn't she? Maybe with the right sort of persuasion she would, but if she didn't, he had to make certain this was the right decision for him.

He noticed a movement beside him and realized that Mike had slipped into a chair vacated by Ashley's youngest sister.

"You look distracted, pal. Everything okay?" Mike asked. "This crowd can be a bit overwhelming the first time you meet them."

"It's not that. I was just thinking about some decisions of my own that need to be made."

"Anything you want to talk about? I'm a good listener. Rick, too."

Josh was startled to find that the prospect of confiding in a couple of male friends held a certain appeal. He'd gone through most of his life with few confidants. Most of his colleagues at the firm had been too competitive to count as friends. Stephanie had filled the role for a while, but this wasn't a decision he could bat around with her. Before he talked to anyone, though, he had to wrestle with it on his own a little longer.

"Another time, okay?"

"Sure," Mike said easily.

"I mean that. I could use another perspective."

"One night next week?"

Josh nodded. "Sounds good to me."

Mike grinned. "I'll set it up with Rick and get back to you. Maybe we can get all the women over to his place and have a guys' night at mine. When you're surrounded by these strong-willed D'Angelo women, it's nice to have backup from time to time." He glanced over at Ashley, then turned back to Josh. "The two of you okay?"

"I thought so, but it's getting complicated."

"That always happens right before the fall."

"The fall?"

"You know, when you tumble head over heels in love."

Josh laughed. "Ah, *that* fall. We're actually way past that point."

"Really?"

"I think I was half in love with her the night she creamed my car." Even as he spoke half in jest, he realized it was true. He did love her.

"When did you fall the rest of the way in love?"

"When she plowed into my boat the next day. She looked so damn vulnerable."

Mike regarded him with surprise. "Ashley? She's the family barracuda."

Josh knew the description was probably apt ninety-nine percent of the time. He'd fallen for Ashley during the one percent when it wasn't. The rest was just a challenge that promised to keep things interesting.

Much as she loved them for coming to Virginia to be supportive, Ashley wished her family would go away. She couldn't think with them underfoot. And the commotion they stirred up with Maggie and Melanie and their husbands dropping by for get-togethers at least once a day kept her from focusing on what she needed to do with the rest of her life.

She was relieved on Sunday night when her parents and Jo announced that they were heading back to Boston first thing in the morning.

"Maggie's going to drive us to the airport," Jo told her.

They sat in the backyard swing enjoying the surprisingly balmy fall night. There wouldn't be many more of them, she was sure.

"Thank you," Ashley said, giving her baby sister a hug. "I know you're responsible for convincing Mom and Dad it's time to go."

Jo chuckled. "You really do owe me. Dad wants to stay and keep an eye on Josh. He thinks there's something fishy about him, no pun intended."

"Why would he think something like that?" Ashley asked.

"He says he can't figure out when the man works. He's sure that's not a good sign."

Ashley was not about to admit that the same thought had crossed her mind, mostly because it didn't speak well of her that she'd shown so little interest in the background of a man with whom everyone could see she was becoming involved.

"Tell Dad not to worry. If things get serious between Josh and me, I'll have him submit a complete résumé for Dad's perusal."

Jo laughed. "You think you're joking. Dad will insist on it."

"It's been good to have you here, baby sister. I've missed you."

"You've only been away for a little over a week, and we've talked almost every day. That's more contact than we have in Boston. You've hardly had time to miss any of us."

"I know," Ashley admitted. "But I like knowing you're close by."

"You'll be home soon," Jo reminded her.

"Maybe," Ashley said, admitting aloud for the first time the possibility that she might not go back to Boston.

Jo stared at her in shock. "Are you saying you might leave Boston for good?"

"Anything's possible," she said.

"Over this? That's ridiculous. You can't let the likes of Wyatt Blake or that awful Tiny Slocum drive you away from your home and family."

"But thanks to them, my reputation's a shambles. It might be smarter to start over somewhere else."

"Such as?"

"Washington, maybe. Richmond. I don't know."

Jo's gaze narrowed. "Here?" she asked. "Because of Josh?"

Ashley refused to be drawn into that discussion again. "I don't know," she repeated emphatically. "I'll keep you posted." She gave her sister a penetrating look. "Meantime, since we have some time to ourselves for a change, why don't you explain why you've been so jumpy every time we've left the house?"

Jo turned surprisingly pale. "I have no idea what you're talking about."

"Of course you do. It's not the first time I've noticed it, either. You were the same way when we came down here to visit Melanie."

"You're imagining things," Jo insisted.

"Did I imagine that you flatly refused to go out for ice cream last night when I know for a fact that you're an ice-cream junkie?"

"I was stuffed from dinner."

Ashley wasn't buying it, but she could tell that she wasn't going to get any answers from her sister. Jo's tight-lipped expression suggested that the conversation was about to erupt into a full-fledged fight if Ashley kept pushing her.

"Okay, I'll back off," she said. "For now. But sweetie, whatever it is, you'd better deal with it. Melanie and Maggie live here now, so coming to Rose Cottage from time to time is inevitable. I don't want you to tense up every time it happens."

"I'll deal with it," Jo said, her expression grim. She stood up abruptly. "I'm going to bed. We have to get an early start in the morning."

"Don't be mad at me for worrying about you," Ashley pleaded.

"How could I be? It's what you do," Jo said, forcing a halfhearted smile.

"Okay, then, good night," Ashley said, giving her a hug, even though Jo didn't return it. "I love you."

Jo sighed. "You, too."

Ashley stared after Jo when she headed upstairs. There was something going on here that none of them knew about. She'd always thought she knew each of her sisters inside out, but it was obvious that Jo was holding back about something. She found that more troubling than if it had been either Maggie or Melanie. They were strong. They had lots of inner resources. Jo was the quiet, sensitive one who took everything to heart. It was apparent to Ashley that something or someone in this town had hurt her baby sister. If she ever figured out what or who that was, there was going to be hell to pay.

Ashley had been so eager to see her family off that she'd barely noticed until they were gone that it was pouring rain. That put a real—and quite literal—damper on her plans to get back into the quiet rhythm of her days with Josh.

Disappointed, she made herself a cup of tea and sat down at the kitchen table. After three days of chaos, she ought to be grateful that she could finally focus on the future. Instead, she felt an inexplicable letdown. She couldn't seem to summon the energy to find one of the legal pads she'd slipped into a drawer where it would be away from her sisters' watchful gazes.

Where was her drive? Where was the sense of urgency she should be feeling? When had she changed so dramatically that all this quiet and solitude no longer made her feel as if she might jump out of her skin? She'd actually started to enjoy the peaceful mornings she spent on the bay with Josh. He didn't press her to talk. Nor did he need to fill every second with the sound of his own voice. He wasn't rushing her to figure things out. She was the one doing that, and she couldn't seem to get started. His quiet, undemanding company was a relief after getting poked and prodded by her family. She'd been looking forward to that today. In fact, she'd been counting on seeing him far more than was probably wise.

When the phone rang a few minutes later and the sound of his voice made her heart skip a bit, she was even more disconcerted.

"Where are you?" he demanded.

"At home, which you should know since you called here. Where are you?"

"In the boat about to head your way."

"Are you crazy? It's pouring outside."

"So? Do you think you're going to melt?"

No, but she would look awful. She had no illusions that soaking-wet hair would do a thing for her. "Maybe the fish need a day off," she said.

And given the little thrill of excitement she'd felt hearing his voice, maybe she needed a day away from Josh to figure out this unexpected attraction that was developing. She couldn't spend her life with some unambitious guy who spent his life fishing to no apparent purpose. This was an interlude. It had to be. Anything else was impossible.

"Okay, then," he said in the easygoing way she found so comforting. "I'll go back in, dry off and pick you up in ten minutes. We'll go into Irvington for breakfast. I know a place that has strong coffee and homemade cinnamon rolls."

Ashley groaned. He'd found her weakness, one she almost never indulged. "Make it fifteen," she said. "I need to hop into the shower and pull myself together."

"I'll give you twenty minutes, then," he teased. "I can't possibly take you out if you're not put together properly."

By the time they reached the coffee shop in nearby Irvington, the sun was fighting its way through the thick gray clouds and the rain was tapering off.

"Want to eat first or explore the shops?" Josh asked.

She studied him with surprise. "A man who likes to shop? I didn't know such a creature existed."

"I couldn't care less about shopping. I just want to see what sort of things make your eyes light up."

Her pulse stuttered at the intensity in his gaze. She could not fall for this man, not right here on the streets of a town hundreds of miles from her home.

"We can start with the cinnamon roll," she said lightly. "After that we'll see how much more of my personality I'm willing to reveal by shopping with you."

When they sat down in the surprisingly crowded coffee shop with its spotless decor and air that was filled with the scent of freshly baked dough and cinnamon, Ashley realized that this felt more like an official date than anything they'd done before. She had coffee dates all the time back home, quick, on-the-run encounters that demanded little more than small talk and served up absolutely no expectations for the way they would end. They gave her the illusion of having a personal life without any of the complications.

Gazing across the table, though, she met Josh's eyes and knew at once that this one was different. It was going to get complicated, simply because her feelings for him had gotten deeper without her even realizing it.

When she finally glanced at Josh, he was watching her as he idly stirred sugar into his coffee. "What?" she asked.

"You seem different this morning."

"Different how?"

"More restless than usual."

"Really? I was thinking earlier about how much I've learned to relax, thanks to you."

He grinned. "You're definitely better than you were, but you seem edgy today. Did something happen with your family?"

"No, not really."

"They got off okay?"

She nodded. "Maggie called from the airport and said their flight was right on time."

"Are they pressuring you to come back to Boston?"

"To be honest, we didn't get into it that much," she admitted. "Every time they brought it up, I cut them off and explained that I have to decide what's right on my own."

"But I imagine they still expressed an opinion or two," he said.

"They're my folks. Of course they want me back home, but they also want me to be happy."

"And for you that means having a successful career," he guessed. "Wherever that might be."

She nodded. "I don't know anything besides law, so I have to go where I can practice."

"Lots of people change careers, if it comes to that," he reminded her.

To her surprise, she said emphatically, "Not me. I want to practice law."

Josh chuckled. "There you go."

"What?" she asked blankly.

"I told you the answers would come to you when you least expect it and when you stop worrying everything to death. You sounded very sure of yourself just then."

Ashley stared at him, then began to grin. "I did, didn't I?"

"Now all you have to decide is where you want to live."

"It may not be that simple," she said, trying to be realistic. "A lot of other firms probably feel the way my old one did. They'll want me but for all the wrong reasons."

"You're obviously an excellent lawyer, if you were able to win an acquittal for a man who turned out to be guilty. You may regret the outcome, but it doesn't change the fact that you did your job very, very well. That's bound to be attractive to a lot of firms."

"That's my point. I don't want a job that's tied to that."

Josh reached for her hand. "Despite the time we've spent together, I can't claim to know you well," he said. "But I think I know enough to say that you care passionately about things. You did what you thought was right at the time in that courtroom. Hindsight is always twenty-twenty, but you have to let the mistakes go or figure out how to rectify them. You can't let them destroy you. That would be a waste."

"I suppose." She wasn't quite ready to get her hopes

up that offers would suddenly start rolling in the minute she let it be known that she was available. At one time that would have been true, but not now.

"Of course, I don't know why I'm trying to encourage you to go back," Josh said, his expression rueful. "It would still suit me just fine if you decided you wanted to open up a private practice right here."

Though she would never in a million years consider such a thing seriously, right here, right now, with his hand on hers and his gaze filled with desire, the idea held a certain appeal.

"Maybe we should just be grateful for the time we have," she said slowly. Yet another answer was coming to her this morning, one that had been in the making since the moment they'd met. She held his gaze. "And maybe we should make better use of it."

The heat in his eyes increased by several degrees. "Shopping's out?"

"It is unless it's the best way you can think of to spend the day."

"Oh, no. I've got all the clutter around my house I need." He gave her a long, intense look. "Want me to show you?"

She grinned, her heart suddenly light, her pulse humming with anticipation. Whatever complications arose because of this decision, she would find a way to live with them. This was about more than having a fling to forget. It was about reaching for something it was no longer possible to resist, something too special to ignore.

"Not as clever as inviting me to look at your etchings, but yes, Josh. The answer is definitely yes."

Chapter Eleven

As they neared his house, Josh tried frantically to recall just how many of his belongings were strewn all over the cottage. Fortunately, he was fairly tidy by nature. He was pretty sure he'd even washed the bowl he'd used for cereal that morning.

Still, he wanted Ashley's first impression of his family's home to be a good one. He'd noticed that the inside of Rose Cottage was immaculate. He imagined that it was much the way it had been before her grandmother's death. He hadn't seen one single personal item that was likely to belong to Ashley. Perhaps that was because she viewed her stay as being so temporary that she'd brought very little with her.

From the outside, Idylwild, which had been in his family for several generations, was very much like Rose

Cottage, at least as Rose Cottage had been back when Cornelia Lindsey had been seeing to its upkeep. He'd noticed lately that though the inside had been painted and the gardens finally manicured after years of neglect, there were still quite a few exterior repairs needed. His own family had been much more conscientious about keeping Idylwild in excellent condition. They'd replaced the old wooden clapboards with vinyl siding, added dark green metal shutters in place of the peeling wooden ones. The only holdover had been the quaint Victorian-trim screen door, which they'd refused to exchange for a more practical storm door.

Inside was a hodgepodge of wicker furniture, oak antiques covered with several layers of paint that had changed with the whims of various occupants and modern appliances in the kitchen. The art on the walls reflected the Madison family's eclectic taste, from ridiculous paintings on driftwood to old watercolors from another era. Oddly enough, it all came together to achieve something cozy and lived-in.

Lately there were a lot more masculine touches, since it had been all but deeded over to him once his parents had moved to Arizona for the drier, warmer air.

Josh stood aside as Ashley entered, and tried to see the small, cluttered living room through her eyes. He had a feeling she preferred cleaner, more modern decor, probably something streamlined and sophisticated.

To his surprise, she immediately smiled and headed straight for a table of old photographs.

"Is there one of you here?" she asked, her curiosity evident.

"Several, more than likely," he admitted, not sure

how eager he was for her to see him as the bespectacled nerd he'd been years ago. Fortunately the table had a lot of photos, many of them of his cousins, most of whom had been far more athletic and handsome than he'd been at sixteen. Given the dramatic changes he'd made physically, he suspected he'd be hard for her to spot.

"Come over here and show me," she said after several minutes of studying and discarding picture after picture.

He grinned at her evident frustration. "No way. You have to try to pick me out of the crowd. Of course, if you can't, I'm not sure whether I'll be insulted or grateful. Meantime, I'll get us some tea, or would you prefer wine?"

"Tea's good."

He left as her brow furrowed in concentration and she picked up each picture and studied it once more.

"Josh, are you sure there's one of you here?" she called out to him eventually.

"Absolutely." He poured the hot water over the tea bags and let them steep, then took the freshly brewed pot and two cups into the living room. "Any luck?"

She was holding a small wood-framed picture and studying it intently. "This one, I think. If I'm right about this one, then there are several more of you, as well."

He walked over. "Let's see." He grinned when he looked at the image of his younger cousin. "Sorry. You lose. That's my cousin Jim."

"But he has your eyes and your mouth," she said. She set the picture back, then met his gaze. "Have I mentioned how much I like your mouth?"

His heart kicked up a notch. "Not that I recall."

"You have very sensual lips." She grinned. "Or maybe I just see them that way because you're such an incredible kisser."

His ego took a satisfying lurch. "Incredible, huh?"

"Mind-boggling, in fact."

Josh leaned down and touched his lips to hers in the slightest brush. "When I kiss you like that?"

"That's nice," she said. "But then there's this other thing you do." She held on to his shirt and skimmed her tongue across his lower lip. "Something like that."

"Ah," he said, nodding. "Like this."

His mouth closed over hers. When her lips parted on a sigh, his tongue invaded. She still had a lingering hint of cinnamon and sugar on her lips, the scent of it on her breath. She was clinging to his shirt, her eyes dazed by the time the kiss ended.

"Mind-boggling," she murmured breathlessly. "Maybe we ought to find that bed before my knees give way."

He laughed. "There's no rush, darlin'. I just made tea."

Her gaze smoldered. "Forget the tea."

Josh swallowed hard. "Forgotten," he said at once, scooping her into his arms.

"How's the rest of your memory? Think you can find your way to the bedroom?"

"There are four bedrooms in this house," he said lightly. "I may not be thinking clearly, but I'm bound to stumble across one of them."

He found his own, of course, and was relieved to find that he'd tossed the covers back in place after yet another restless night. When he lowered Ashley to her feet beside the bed, he very nearly had to pinch himself to be sure this moment wasn't a dream. He wouldn't go so far as to say he'd had a crush on her forever, because it hadn't been like that. It had been impossible—at least for him—to fantasize about anything real with a girl who was so far beyond his reach.

But he'd wondered about her, wondered about all of the D'Angelo girls who were always laughing, always having spirited adventures with the most popular boys in town. The reality, as it turned out, was better than anything he'd imagined. This flesh-and-blood woman made him long for things he'd never expected to want so much…a home, a family, a future that didn't involve nonstop work to get ahead. He'd never had those thoughts as a teenager. Nor had he had them as recently as last week when he'd still been debating taking things to the next level with Stephanie.

Ashley, however, promised to provide endless fascination. As a girl, from his vantage point of distance and teenaged longing, she'd seemed strong, intelligent and invincible to him. She was all of those things as a woman, but she was also vulnerable, and that made her seem accessible in ways he'd never dared to dream about.

She touched him, then, her fingers grazing the bare skin of his chest, then dipping lower. The memories fled, replaced by a sea of sensations in the here-and-now. Need exploded inside him, but patience—years of it, or so it seemed—kept his hands steady and slow.

She didn't seem to want slow, though. She moved restlessly against him, taunting him deliberately, moving aside his careful fingers to strip away clothing in an anxious rush. She barely gave him time to appreciate her naked beauty before she was pulling him onto the bed.

Josh was no fool. As much as he wanted to linger

over every caress, to savor every touch, he caught on to her edgy, almost desperate mood and gave her what she wanted. He pinned her hands loosely above her head, then looked into her eyes, searching for her soul. It was there when he entered her with one hard thrust, all the need, all the desire, all the raw wanting that any man could ask for.

She came apart at once, shuddering beneath him, surrounding him with slick, pulsing heat. He smiled into her eyes.

"That one was for you, darlin'."

She gave him a lazy, satisfied smile of her own. "And now?"

"And now we're going to do this again," he said.

"Oh, really?"

"And this time it will be for both of us."

He waited for her body to grow still, waited for the longing to rise once more in her eyes and then he began to move, slowly at first, letting the sweet tension build, until she was pleading with him for yet another release.

"In time," he murmured. "In good time."

Given her penchant for control, he wasn't surprised when her body tried to take the decisions away from him, but he was more determined. He held her in place, his rock-hard arousal sheathed in her, not moving a muscle until she calmed, her gaze alert and filled with interest in what he had planned.

Satisfied that he had her full and captivated attention, he began to move again, this time responding to her little cries of pleasure with deeper, harder thrusts until the rhythm was no longer his—or hers—to control. They were both caught up in the passion, in the frantic need.

He was pretty sure they were going to go up in flames, if something didn't happen to lessen the mounting heat, the sweet, powerful friction that was driving them wild.

Josh had no idea what it would take to send them flying, but he hadn't expected it to be a smile. Ashley's lips curved ever so slightly into a Mona Lisa smile of purest satisfaction and he came undone. The smile spread as she came with him.

As they slowly fell back to earth, Josh cradled her against his chest and fell into the deepest, most contented sleep of his life, only barely resisting the urge to whisper that he'd fallen in love with her. Only the shock of that, the wonder, kept him silent. That and the fear that even after what they'd just shared, she wouldn't feel the same way.

"Do you have any idea how intimidated I was by you?" Josh asked Ashley as they lay side by side in his bed after making love for yet a third time during the long, lazy afternoon. The rain had started once again and was beating a staccato rhythm on the old tin roof.

Taken aback, Ashley stared at him. Of all the things he'd said and done since they met, this was the one that most astonished her. "Intimidated? Why?"

"Because you're one of the totally unattainable D'Angelo sisters, the most beautiful, most intelligent one. When I was sixteen, I never in a million years would have dreamed we'd be together like this."

She was even more astounded by that. "You knew me when you were sixteen?"

He laughed. "Hardly. I knew *of* you. Every boy in three counties knew who you were. You and your sisters breezed in here every summer and left behind a trail of broken hearts each fall. Your poor grandmother was constantly apologizing to all the mothers." He regarded her intently. "Is that what you're going to do to me? Will I wind up being your autumn fling?"

His tone was light, but Ashley heard the note of real concern behind it. "You know I can't make any guarantees right now, Josh. This is what it is, for as long as it lasts. We have to agree to that, or it's pointless to even start."

He gave her a wry look and ran a hand over her hip. "I'd say we've already started."

Indeed, they had. Ashley hadn't felt this way in a long time. Her body was still quaking inside from the power of what they'd just shared. And based on the shiver that Josh's light touch had just sent over her, she was eager to try it again. Before she could indulge herself, though, she wanted him to explain how they'd never met.

"Why didn't we know each other back then?" she asked him, tracing the outline of his wickedly clever mouth. "It's not as if we were living miles and miles apart."

"You and your sisters were way out of my league," he said with a self-deprecating smile. "It was sort of like the difference between standard-issue white bread and one of those crusty loaves of olive bread that come from a gourmet bakery. No comparison."

Her gaze narrowed. "Are you saying we were snobs?" The possibility rankled, most likely because she feared there might be some truth to it. Look at the judgments she'd been making about men her entire adult life. Look at how stunned she'd been that Josh had slipped past the careful screening system that tended to weed out anyone she deemed unsuitable by some ridiculous standard that combined ambition and success to the exclusion of character.

He shook his head. "Not at all. I just wasn't on your radar. That's obvious, since you couldn't pick out my picture from those photos in the living room. I was the one with glasses and a pained smile."

She immediately remembered a picture that had charmed her. The boy, barely a teenager, had looked miserably self-conscious as he gazed at the camera. "I know exactly which picture it is," she said. "Wait."

She scrambled from the bed and ran to get it. "This is you," she said, holding it out to him when she'd returned.

He winced as he looked at it, then nodded. "That's me, all right."

"You were a cutie," she said.

"Please. If you believe that, then you have a very broad definition of the word."

"You were a cutie," she repeated. "I can't believe I never spotted you."

"That was as much my fault as yours. I was shy and got along better with the characters in books than I did with real-life girls my own age."

"That's amazing," she said.

"What? That I turned into this sexy stud muffin?"

Ashley couldn't contain the laugh that bubbled up. "No, that I missed knowing you back then. I've always had a thing for shy bookworms."

Josh scoffed at her. "Kenny Foster was about as far from a shy bookworm as this region ever produced."

She blinked at the mention of a name long forgotten.

"Kenny Foster," she repeated. "My gosh, whatever happened to him?"

"You didn't keep up with him?"

"Obviously not."

Josh grinned. "Just as well. You'd have had to defend him on an embezzling charge. His fingers got a little sticky down at the bank."

"You're kidding! My dad always said he had shifty eyes."

"Your dad's obviously a very wise man."

She met his gaze. "Want to know what he says about you?"

His expression sobered. "I don't know. Do I?"

"He thinks there's something fishy about a man who never goes to work."

To her surprise Josh didn't seem to take offense.

"If only he knew," he said dryly.

"Knew what?"

"That this is the first time off I've taken in five years."

She studied him with surprise. "Really?"

"No lie."

"Me, too," she said, holding up her hand to give him a high five. "I don't suppose you're having the same kind of career crisis I'm having, though."

"I wouldn't call it a crisis," he said. "Just thinking about a few things."

She sat up beside him. Now was her chance to return the favor and listen to him, just as he'd allowed her to go on and on. "Talk to me."

He shook his head. "I have the woman of my dreams in my bed and you want to do career counseling? I don't think so."

"What did you want to do?"

"This," he said, reaching for her.

When his mouth closed over hers, all thoughts of jobs and just about everything else flew out the window. He was right. Why waste time on anything else, when there were so many sensations they had yet to share?

"Where exactly were you all day yesterday?" Maggie asked when Ashley finally returned her call the next morning after she got home from Josh's. "I called three times after I got back from dropping everyone off at the airport."

"I know. I got the messages."

"And I dropped by the house."

"Doesn't surprise me a bit," Ashley said.

"Well?"

"Well, what?"

"Oh, stop it, were you with Josh or not?"

"None of your business."

"Which means you were," Maggie concluded. "Just how serious are things getting between the two of you?"

Ashley didn't have a good answer to that. The sex was definitely serious. In fact, it was magnificent. She couldn't say the same about the relationship. There were some huge gaps that needed to be filled in before she could honestly say they had one.

"I can't answer that."

"Can't or won't?"

"Does it matter?" she asked irritably.

"Yes, it matters. I'm coming over. We obviously need to talk."

"We do not need to talk. And I don't want you and

Melanie to get the idea that you need to start planning the wedding."

"I should hope not," Maggie said so emphatically that it caught Ashley off guard.

"I thought you liked Josh."

"I do. We all do. In fact, all the guys are going over to Melanie's tonight to bond over beer and burgers, which is why I was calling you. Melanie and I want you to join us here."

"Why? Are you serving beer and burgers, too?"

"Please. I'm the sister who cooks, remember? I'm serving roasted pork with apricot sauce, mashed potatoes and an asparagus salad. Melanie's bringing a decadent chocolate cake."

"Do the men know about this meal? It might make them rethink the whole beer-and-burgers thing."

"I think it's more about the bonding than the menu," Maggie told her. "And I've instructed Rick not to come home without a few answers about the mysterious Josh Madison."

"Meaning?"

"We all like him, but what do we really know about him?"

"About as much as you knew about Rick before you climbed into bed with him," Ashley reminded her tartly.

"Ha-ha," Maggie retorted. "But I learned a whole lot more before I agreed to marry him."

"I haven't agreed to marry Josh."

"Then the subject has come up?" Maggie said, seizing on Ashley's inadvertent slip of the tongue.

"In passing," she admitted. "But do you honestly think I'd consider spending my life with a guy I hardly know?"

"Not without running his Dun and Bradstreet rating," Maggie said. "Have you done that?"

"No, I have not done that," Ashley said, wounded yet again by the suggestion that her standards for men were suspect. "In fact, that's insulting. I'm not a snob."

"Not a snob, just very certain of the kind of man you want in your life. Are you telling me you no longer care about the designer apparel and the Rolex watch?"

"It's never been about the damn clothes," she snapped, even though Josh's wardrobe had been one of the first things she'd noticed. It hadn't impressed her. Lately, though, she'd hardly noticed what he wore. It simply hadn't mattered.

"No, it's been about the man having enough ambition to be able to afford them," Maggie agreed. "Maybe I've missed something. What does Josh actually do for a living? Do you know something about his career that the rest of us don't?"

"No, I'm not entirely sure, either. I do know that he's thinking of making a change, same as me."

"Great, two of you in career crisis. That ought to provide a nice solid foundation for marriage."

"Go to hell," Ashley said, losing patience with the whole conversation, mostly because she didn't have any of the answers about Josh she probably should have, given the increasing intensity of her feelings for him. She didn't do anything impulsively, yet she'd managed to get involved with a virtual stranger in barely more than a week. And, like it or not, she was involved with him.

"We'll discuss this some more tonight. I'll see you at seven," Maggie said sweetly.

"I never said I was coming."

"But you will."

"Oh? Why is that?"

"Because you know if you don't, Melanie and I will be on your doorstep by seven ten."

"Fine. Whatever."

"I mean it, big sister. You need a plan of action. You need to find out who Josh is before you get any more deeply involved with him."

"Now who's being a snob? Isn't it enough that he's been amazingly supportive and kind? Isn't it enough that he's smart and fun, to say nothing of sexy?"

Maggie chuckled. "Nice defense for a woman who's only casually interested in the guy. We'll talk some more about that, too."

"I can't tell you how I'm looking forward to it," Ashley said sarcastically and hung up.

If she had half a brain, she'd stay as far away from her sister's tonight as she possibly could. Unfortunately, unless she hid out in another state, Maggie and Melanie wouldn't hesitate to track her down. No, it was better to go and save all of them the trouble. She'd just perfect her technique for saying *no comment* to anything she didn't care to answer.

Chapter Twelve

Josh studied the uneasy expressions on Mike's and Rick's faces and concluded that he was about to be served up along with the burgers. "Okay, guys, what's the deal?"

They were surprisingly reticent. Mike flipped the hamburgers on the grill and avoided looking at him directly. Rick sighed.

"I'm waiting," he prodded.

"We're on a mission," Rick finally admitted. "From our wives," he added, as if there were any question about who'd put them up to it.

Josh bit back a chuckle at the idea of these two men, both of whom obviously had a very strong sense of who they were, being manipulated by the women in their lives. It was a testament to how deeply they loved their wives. "Interesting. And you felt obligated to accept this mission?"

"Oh, yeah," Mike confirmed. "If I were you, I'd run right now. The list of very intrusive questions we were given is endless." He reached in his pocket and pulled out a wrinkled piece of paper. "Melanie made notes. She didn't trust my memory."

Rick held out a similar sheet of paper. "Neither did Maggie." He frowned at Mike. "I think we were supposed to be more subtle about it."

Josh laughed. "You definitely missed the boat on that. Doesn't matter, though. I'm afraid I can't hide from a few questions," he said with some regret. "It would send the wrong message, don't you think?"

"That's what I said," Rick commented. "Once those two scent blood, they'll be all over you like a couple of hound dogs. You can forget about pursuing Ashley. Maggie and Melanie will take up all your time, pestering you with the same questions, making your life a living hell. We're your best bet. At least with us, you'll have sympathetic male ears."

"Yeah, I can see that," Josh said wryly. "I don't suppose there's any chance at all that you can just tell them I'm a great guy and let it go at that?"

"Fat chance," Mike said. "It's details they're after. They think you're keeping a lot of deep, dark secrets from Ashley."

"Nothing important," he assured them. "But I suppose my word on that isn't enough."

"Afraid not," Rick said apologetically.

Josh took a long swallow of his beer, then sat down

in one of the Adirondack chairs on the deck. "Okay, go for it. Ask whatever you want to."

"Maybe we should at least wait till after you've eaten," Mike suggested, obviously not at all anxious to get started. "These are going to be outstanding burgers. I'd hate to ruin your appetite. And a couple of beers from now, the inquisition won't be quite so painful."

Josh shrugged. He was in no hurry to get into this discussion. "Works for me. And make it two burgers. I'd like to put this off as long as possible, too." He turned to Rick. "Did you really have this much trouble with the sisters when you were courting Maggie?"

"To tell you the truth, the sisters were great," Rick confided. "Maggie was the tough sell. She thought it was all about the sex. She figured the fire would burn itself out eventually and we'd have nothing."

Josh lifted a brow. "But it wasn't about the sex?"

"Well, sure it was, at first," Rick admitted. "I'd played a very gorgeous field for a very long time. Done it damn well, too. I couldn't imagine myself settling down."

"What changed?" Josh asked.

"Maggie ran. Naturally, since no woman had ever done that to me before, I came after her. She still didn't trust me or what we had. I fought. She resisted. It didn't take long for me to weigh settling down against a future without Maggie. I realized very quickly that it was no contest. Once I got to that point, marriage was the obvious answer."

"And that took how long?" Josh asked.

"A few weeks."

"Same with me," Mike said. "My first marriage had pretty much been a disaster. I wasn't looking for a wife, especially with Jessie wildly out of control. I'll be grateful till the end of my days that Melanie looked beyond the mess we were in and took us on. She's made everything since then seem easy."

Mike handed each of them a burger, then sat down with his own. After he'd taken a couple of bites, he glanced slyly at Josh. "Why are you so interested? Are you thinking about marrying Ashley?"

"It's crossed my mind a time or two," Josh admitted. "Like I told you before, though, there are a lot of issues that need to be resolved before either one of us could take the idea seriously. Ashley's career means a lot to her and it's pretty messed up. She needs to work that out. She's not entirely sure who she is or what she wants right now. Me, I think it's clear what she ought to do, but it's not my opinion that counts."

"You could steer her in the right direction," Mike reminded him. "Make the idea of relocating her practice here irresistible."

"I've planted the idea in her head, but so far she's been fairly resistant."

The two men exchanged a look that Josh couldn't interpret. "What?" he asked.

"Maybe you should offer to go into practice with her," Rick suggested casually.

Josh choked on his beer. "Excuse me?"

Mike grinned. "Hard to keep a secret like that in a town this small. Ever since you showed up, I've been running into people who've been only too happy to tell me how lucky I am to have such a successful lawyer for a neighbor. Seems a lot of these folks read the Richmond papers. Lucky for you, Melanie hasn't gotten wind of it yet."

"Neither has Maggie," Rick added. "What I can't figure out is why you'd want to keep it quiet from Ashley. You haven't told her, have you?"

Josh shook his head. "I know it doesn't make a lot of sense, but the night we met she made some crack about me obviously not being a lawyer since I wasn't ready to sue her for damages after that accident. Since I'd been wrestling with whether to change careers or at least leave my firm in Richmond, I sort of went along with her. I figured I could use a break from the whole big-time lawyer image. It was only later, when I realized just how deep her own issues with the law ran, that I saw how stupid it had been not to tell her in the first place. Now I'm not sure how she's going to take it." He regarded them hopefully. "She could be thrilled to discover we have that in common, couldn't she?"

Rick chuckled. "She could be, but my guess is she's going to be mad as a hornet."

"I agree," Mike added. "I'm no expert, but I have figured out that women don't like being lied to."

"It wasn't a lie," Josh said. "It was an omission."

"Well, pardon us all to hell," Rick said, obviously amused. "An omission." He nodded sagely. "Yes, indeed. Explain it just that way. I'm sure that'll make all the difference."

Josh sighed at the grim reality check. "Okay, okay, she's going to be furious."

"Add in the fact that her client lied to her, her boss at the law firm betrayed her and, according to Melanie, her last relationship ended because of a lie, I think furious is putting it mildly," Mike added.

Josh looked from one man to the other and decided it was definitely time to cast pride aside and plead for help. "What the hell do I do now?"

"Grovel," Rick suggested cheerfully.

"Get the truth out there and *then* grovel," Mike corrected.

"I'm not sure I know how," Josh said. He'd never had to grovel before in his life. But to save what he had with Ashley, he was willing to give it a try. "Do I start with flowers?"

Rick laughed. "You are so pathetic. I seem to recall being exactly like you, right, Mike?"

"You were pitiful," Mike concurred.

"Not helping, guys," Josh said. "Clue me in on the groveling thing. I've never had to do it before."

"Send flowers and candy," Mike suggested. "Take over wine and candles and dinner."

"No, no, no," Rick protested. "You have to remember who she is."

Josh stared at him blankly. "I thought all women loved the whole flowers and candy business."

"They do, but keep in mind what's important to Ashley. Buy her a briefcase or the latest handheld computer gadget. Buy her a shingle for a law office."

"Hey, I like that one," Josh said.

"Just don't make it Madison and D'Angelo on the sign," Mike recommended. "D'Angelo and Madison is better. Aside from getting top billing, she'll think she has the upper hand."

Josh laughed. "She does have the upper hand. She has since the day we met."

He didn't see that changing in this lifetime, not as

long as he continued to be completely dazzled by her. He pretty much expected that would last forever.

"How could you, of all people, get so deeply involved with a man you barely know?" Maggie asked, regarding Ashley incredulously. "You pride yourself on digging beneath the surface, scrambling all over for every bit of evidence in a case that could exonerate a client. Didn't you stop for one single second and ask yourself what you really knew about Josh before you climbed into bed with him?"

Trying not to feel foolish, Ashley shook her head. "He was just sort of there. It's not as if we were really dating. We literally drifted into spending time together. It was fun and uncomplicated, at least at the beginning. I didn't want a lot of information. I didn't figure I needed it, since I was going to go back to Boston in three weeks and probably never see him again. Besides, he wasn't my type."

"As if tall, dark and gorgeous isn't everyone's type," Melanie scoffed.

"That barely registered," Ashley admitted.

"Because you didn't think he was polished enough or ambitious enough," Maggie guessed.

Ashley sighed at how that made her look, but it was true. Dammit, she was a snob, after all. "Okay, yes," she admitted. "He seemed to lack some of the essentials that have always been important to me."

"And now?" Melanie asked, regarding her sympathetically.

"And now it's gotten complicated," Ashley said. "Those things don't seem to matter quite so much."

"How so?" Melanie asked.

"She's fallen for him," Maggie replied before Ashley could say a word. "She's slept with him, the sex was fantastic and now she has stars in her eyes that enable her to overlook his possible lack of a bank account or decent wardrobe of designer suits and Italian shoes."

Ashley frowned at her. "You're one to talk about falling in lust, then falling in love. Wasn't that precisely how it was with you and Rick? Isn't that exactly why you hightailed it out of Boston—because you were falling for him because the sex was good?"

"Great," Maggie corrected. "The sex was incredible." She grinned. "Still is, in case you were wondering."

Ashley groaned. "Too much information."

Melanie chuckled. "Besides, she wants us to stay focused on her."

"Trust me, not so much," Ashley retorted. "We could drop this entire subject and it wouldn't bother me a bit. I can deal with my personal life on my own."

"Obviously," Maggie said. "That's why you know so much about the man you're sleeping with."

"You don't have to be sarcastic," Ashley told her.

"I think I do," Maggie said. "This isn't like you at all, big sister. It's a recipe for disaster. You need to start asking some questions. What if you find out he just got out of jail?"

"Don't be ridiculous," Ashley said, then realized she truly didn't know enough to dispute the possibility. And her judgment hadn't been sharp enough to recognize a murderer when he'd been sitting right next to her for weeks. Who knew what secrets Josh might be keeping? He seemed so down-to-earth and sincere, she couldn't imagine that there was a dark side lurking somewhere inside him, but she couldn't swear it didn't exist. That was worrisome.

"Okay, I promise I'll sit down and have a heart-to-heart with him before this goes any further."

Maggie studied her with a narrowed gaze. "How much further is it going to go? All of this could be moot, if you're going back to Boston soon."

Ashley sighed. "I don't know if I am or not," she told them. "And I really, really don't want to discuss that tonight. I've made a promise to myself that first thing tomorrow I'm going to sit down and start making a list of my options."

"Is staying here one of them?" Melanie asked.

"It'll be on the list," Ashley conceded. "But not near the top. It'll be there because I can't afford to dismiss anything out of hand."

"Will it be on there at all because you like the idea at least a little or because of Josh?" Maggie asked.

"What difference does it make?" Ashley replied.

Her sisters exchanged a knowing glance. It was Melanie who answered. "A big one, I would think," she told Ashley. "Whatever you decide, it has to be what's best for you. Josh shouldn't even enter into it. Not unless you're more serious about him than you're letting on."

"It's complicated," Ashley said again. She was crazy about him, but she didn't want to be, didn't think she should be. In fact, if she had an excuse, any excuse at all, she'd disentangle herself from the relationship and flee back to Boston. As bad and as unpredictable as her professional life there was, it was a whole lot easier to understand than the current roller-coaster ride of her emotions.

She stood up. "I'm going home," she announced. She didn't bother explaining that the home she intended to run to was in Boston. She needed to get her emotional feet back under her.

"We haven't even had dessert," Melanie protested. "You have to stay for chocolate cake."

"Not tonight," Ashley said. She gave each of her sisters a fierce hug. "Thanks for helping me to get a clearer picture of all this."

Maggie looked surprised. "We actually helped?"

"Yes, brat. You helped. You, too, Melanie. I think I know exactly what I need to do next."

But she had to make one important stop before she left town. She had to see Josh and try to explain why she was bailing on him and everything that had been building between them.

Ashley had forgotten about the whole guy-bonding session. When she got to Josh's, the house was dark. She could leave him a note, try to explain her decision without having to bear the disappointment that was bound to be in his eyes, but when she really thought about it, she knew she couldn't take the coward's way out. If nothing else, she owed him for being there for her during the worst days of her life.

Since it was a mild enough night, she left the car and went to wait for him on the porch. She was idly rocking when his car finally turned off the road and pulled to a stop.

"Hey," he said, his tone cautious as he approached. "I wasn't expecting you to be here."

"Is it okay?"

"Of course." He dropped a light kiss on her forehead, then leaned against the porch railing. "How was your evening with your sisters?"

"About as much fun as walking barefoot through glass. How about yours with the guys?"

"Interesting," he said in a way that made her instantly alert.

"What did they say?"

"I'll tell you in a minute," he promised, lifting her out of the rocker, then settling in it himself with her on his lap. "Much better."

Ashley linked her arms around his neck and rested her forehead against his. "I missed you tonight," she admitted, surprising herself. It wasn't what she'd intended to say at all. She'd planned to keep the conversation cool and impersonal, explain that she had to leave town, had to figure things out without him to distract her. Now she couldn't seem to summon the words.

"That's a good thing, isn't it?" Josh asked, studying her worriedly.

"In a way, I suppose."

"Then why do you look so sad? Were your sisters that hard on you?"

"They worry about me, that's all. They're not convinced I'm thinking clearly these days." She shrugged. "They could be right. At the very least, they gave me some things to think about."

"Such as?"

"I don't want to get into it," she said. Talk wasn't what she needed now. She wanted to feel the way only this man had ever made her feel…cherished. "Make love to me, Josh, please."

He searched her face. "You sure we don't need to have a long talk first? I know your sisters were probably plaguing you with questions about me, since that's what their husbands were doing to me. I figure they'll spend the rest of the night comparing notes. Don't you feel a need to be as up to speed as your sisters will be?"

"Eventually," she said. "But right now I want to be in your arms."

"Happy to oblige," he said. "But then I think we'd better talk about this evening."

"Yours or mine?"

"Both," he said, sounding serious.

"Okay," she agreed reluctantly, then brightened. "Maybe if we go inside and make intense, passionate love, we'll forget what we wanted to talk about."

He grinned. "You do have the ability to make me forget my own name from time to time."

She met his gaze, for some reason needing more. She wanted to know that she made him half as crazy as he made her. "Only from time to time?" she taunted.

"Okay, most of the time," he responded, a glint of knowing amusement in his eyes. "Is it vital that you know how much power you have over me?"

It had been, but now it scared her, especially since she knew what she had to do. She touched his cheek. "I'm not sure I want to have power over you."

"Why?"

"Because that means I could hurt you."

"You won't hurt me, Ashley." He sighed, looking sad. "If anything, it will be the other way around."

She was shocked by his assessment. "You've been wonderful to me," she protested.

"I've tried to be. I've wanted to be," he said. "But I'm not perfect."

She wanted to put a smile back in his eyes, so she said, "Next best thing to perfect, then. Besides, perfection is highly overrated."

"I hope you go on thinking that forever," he said in a way that told her he was sure it would be otherwise.

Ashley swallowed hard. Hadn't she warned herself just a short time ago that this was going to get increasingly complicated? She was beginning to think she might have underestimated just how complicated it could be. Maybe it needed to be reduced to the basics, at least one last time. Maybe that would help her to clarify her feelings before she went back to the relative safety of Boston to think things through. Instead of providing a safe haven, Rose Cottage had only placed her in the middle of a deeper quagmire.

"We're talking too much," she told him.

He hesitated, then nodded. "Entirely too much."

He stood up with her cradled against his chest and went inside, then kicked the door closed behind them.

This time they never made it to the bedroom. There was something almost desperate pulling them together, making each caress as wickedly hot as a flame, making their coming together as explosive as dynamite.

Kisses stole breath. Touches tormented. Clothes flew in every direction as they tumbled onto the sofa in a mad frenzy, arms and legs tangled, bodies uniting.

Ashley shuddered as wave after wave of pleasure crashed over her, taking her under to a dark, dangerous place where only Josh mattered. She lost herself in him and then, when a climax ripped through her, found herself again in his eyes.

It was the first time in her life she'd fully understood the meaning of magic and why women craved it.

Chapter Thirteen

Josh woke up to find the other side of his bed empty. He should have been accustomed to the feeling, but it felt lonely somehow after having Ashley in his arms for most of the night. He shivered in the chilly air, then dragged on a pair of sweatpants and a T-shirt and went hunting for the woman who'd spent the entire night making his heart pound and his blood race. He doubted he would ever get enough of her.

But today could change everything, he warned himself. Once he told her the truth about his career, about all of the issues that had brought him to Idylwild and that he had kept from her, she might walk out of his life. The prospect made his heart ache. He simply couldn't allow it to happen. He would fight with everything in him to see that she understood his reticence and forgave him.

First, though, he had to find the words and the courage to utter them.

"Hey, beautiful, where are you?" he called out, heading for the kitchen and the aroma of freshly brewed coffee.

When she didn't respond, his heart began to thud. Despite her silence, he sensed that she was still in the house, which meant something was very wrong.

"Ashley!"

Again, nothing.

He found her standing by his dining room table, where he'd been doing some work the day before. It had become his makeshift office, which meant there were papers there that could have given him away. He knew in an instant that that was exactly what had happened.

She was staring out the window. Though the sun was glistening on the bay just outside, he had a sick feeling that it wasn't the beauty of the view that had made her so still. He knew in his gut that the revelation he'd intended to make was now out of his hands. She knew.

"Ashley?"

She turned slowly, an expression of hurt and betrayal written all over her face. Whatever slim hope he'd held out that there was still time for him to tell her everything himself vanished.

"What is it?" he asked, praying that he'd gotten it wrong. "What's happened?"

"I was looking for some paper to make a list," she whispered. "I found this instead." She held up a piece of stationery—letterhead from his firm—in a hand that trembled visibly. "You're a lawyer," she said as if it were some sort of crime. "You're with a very prestigious firm, in fact."

"Yes," he admitted, knowing the wounded expression in her eyes would haunt him forever. "I'm an attorney."

She shook her head as if she still couldn't quite believe it. "I don't understand, Josh. Why didn't you tell me? That first night, when I made that crack about you definitely not being a lawyer, why didn't you say right then that I had it all wrong? All this time, when you were so sympathetic to me, you could have told me that you understood because you know firsthand what it's like, but you never once said that. Why not? Why keep it a secret?"

"Because at that moment, I didn't want to be a lawyer anymore. I liked that you thought I was something else."

"That doesn't make any sense," she said impatiently. "Are you ashamed of it for some reason? Are you one of those lawyers who bends the rules, does whatever it takes to win, the kind you described with such disdain? Is that why you didn't think there was anything wrong with the way I handled Tiny Slocum's case?"

"It wasn't about you, Ashley. And, yes, sometimes I am ashamed of being a lawyer," he admitted. "And like you, I've spent a lot of time lately wondering about the path I'm on. Not for the same reasons, of course, but it's still an identity crisis and, frankly, I was no more ready to talk about it than you were to talk about your situation. I came here to think, to make some tough choices. You know my philosophy on all that. I mull things over, push them to the back of my mind until the answer finally makes its way through the chaos. I'm not like you. I don't worry it to death, make lists, debate the pros and cons."

"Not even with me? I thought I mattered to you."

"You did," he said. "You do. It wasn't about you. It was about me."

"But you had to know I had issues about people lying to me. There were a dozen different times when you could have told me and you didn't," she protested. "Why hide it, especially after I'd told you what was going on with me? All you had to do was say, 'Hey, Ashley, I'm a lawyer, so I get what you're going through.' Period. That's it. If you didn't want to talk about your issues, fine. I could have understood that."

"I see that now," he said honestly. "I see that keeping it from you was wrong, that I turned it into a big deal when it shouldn't have mattered at all. And I can tell you that I regret staying silent. It was foolish and unfair. Rick and Mike made me see that last night."

"They know?" she asked incredulously. "You told them before you told me?"

"No. I didn't have to tell them. Apparently several people in town had mentioned it to them. They confronted me about it last night, told me that I was being an idiot for not telling you, that I was putting your trust at risk. That's why I wanted to talk when I got back here and found you waiting. I knew I'd kept silent too long, that you had to know before you found out some other way."

"Too little too late," she said disdainfully. "You made a fool of me," she whispered. "Just like before, and once again I never saw it coming. What is wrong with me? How did I turn into such a lousy judge of character?"

"Ashley, it's not as if I've committed a crime or kept another woman from you. Law is a job, and at the time I wasn't very happy with it."

"But it's who you are. Now I have to question whether I ever really knew you."

"You do," he argued. "You know everything important."

He reached for her, but she pulled away. Fighting the panic clawing at him when he realized he really could lose her over this, he tried to explain. "It just didn't matter, Ashley, especially when being a lawyer was something I was questioning anyway. Why does what I do for a living matter so much to you, anyway?"

"That's not the point," she said defensively. "You lied. That's what I care about."

He studied her curiously. He had a feeling she wasn't being entirely honest herself. His career did matter to her in some way he had yet to discern. "What did you think I did for a living?"

She hesitated then, her turmoil evident. "I wasn't sure. Fished maybe."

Josh laughed at the absurdity of that. "You must have thought I was damned bad at it. The biggest catch we brought in was three rockfish, and *you* caught those."

Her defensiveness came back. "I figured since you were on vacation, that you weren't really trying."

He regarded her skeptically and waited.

She sighed, then admitted, "Okay, it felt safe that you were nothing more than some halfway idle guy."

His heart sank as he realized what she was really saying. "Because you could never fall for a man like that, right? A man with no ambition?"

She nodded, looking miserable. "I'm sorry. I know that sounds insulting."

"It *is* insulting, especially considering what went on here last night and on at least one other occasion. If you think what I did was so awful, think about how it makes me feel to know that essentially you were using me to scratch some itch, that you figured a mere fisherman couldn't be hurt by whatever game you were playing."

She looked as if he'd slapped her. "It wasn't like that, Josh."

"Really? Then how was it? Please explain it, because right this second I'm pretty sure I feel like an even bigger fool than you do."

"I was falling for you," she insisted.

"Despite me being some unsuccessful fisherman," he said sarcastically, letting his fury reach a boil. Everything was falling apart and anger was just about the only thing that was going to get him through the pain of it. "How gracious of you to look beyond my lowly lifestyle. How did I miss the fact that you are such a snob?"

"I'm sorry." She scraped a hand through her thick hair, leaving it more tousled than ever.

Josh had to tear his gaze away. That was the way he liked her best, looking sexily rumpled and accessible. He couldn't let himself think of her that way now. He had to hang on to his outrage.

"I guess we're both lucky," he said.

"Lucky?" she repeated incredulously. "How do you figure that?"

"We've just avoided making a horrible mistake. I thought I was in love with a brilliant, generous-hearted woman. You thought you were falling for a guy who was good in bed and nothing more. Turns out we were both wrong." He met her gaze. "I guess the reality isn't nearly as appealing as the fantasy."

She winced at that. "I should go," she said, then waited, almost as if she were hoping that he'd try to stop her.

He didn't say a word. He couldn't. He could only

think about the irony of this whole mess. He'd been falling in love with her and she'd been using him for easy, uncomplicated sex. That was definitely a turnabout in his life. One of these days when it stopped hurting so damn much, he might even laugh about it.

Ashley drove back to Rose Cottage in a daze. How had everything spun so wildly out of control in little more than a heartbeat? She wished she'd never found the stupid letter, never discovered that Josh was a lawyer.

Maybe in another hour, he would have told her himself. It would have shaken her, but at least the news would have come from him. Maybe that alone would have been enough to redeem him, so they could go on together.

"Don't be ridiculous," she told herself as she went inside and made herself a cup of tea. She would have been just as angry, felt just as betrayed, if the announcement had tripped off his lips. His being a lawyer was a big deal. His hiding it from her was an even bigger one. She simply couldn't stomach being with another person who couldn't tell her the truth. How could anyone be expected to build a relationship on lies and half-truths?

She sat at the kitchen table, sipping her tea and trying to work up the energy to pack for the return to Boston. It didn't seem half as urgent to run back home now. The decision about what to do about Josh and her feelings for him had been made. It was a nonissue. They were over. Even if she weren't furious at him for the lie, he would probably never forgive her for the judgments she'd made about him.

As for the whole question of her professional future,

she could just as easily decide that sitting right here at the kitchen table.

Determined to get on with it, she pushed aside her emotions and retrieved a yellow legal pad and a handful of pens. Just spreading them on the table in front of her immediately made her feel better, more in control. Making lists was something she excelled at doing. She liked being organized and practical. It was about time she remembered that. Idle mulling might work for Josh, but it simply wasn't her way. It was ridiculous. Decisions that were made like that couldn't be trusted. They were little more than impulse. She liked her decisions to be based on sound logic and clear thinking.

Okay, then, she thought, she had four basic choices.

First, she could go back to Boston and begin applying at other law firms. Under that she jotted down a couple of quick notes on the positive side; that she would be near her family and that she had a reputation in Boston. She sighed and put that reputation down as a negative, too. It was hard to tell which way that one would go, to her advantage or her disadvantage.

Next, she listed the option of looking for jobs in other cities, such as Richmond or Washington. More negatives than positives immediately popped into mind. It would mean relocating to cities where she knew no one, taking the bar exam again, being separated from her family. Those were all huge, though not insurmountable, drawbacks. On the plus side, such a decision would offer a new challenge, a fresh start. There was a lot to be said for that.

Or, she wrote down, she could change careers entirely. She was a bright woman with many interests she had yet to fully explore. She could certainly find some way to utilize those skills and talents to find a whole new direction for her life. She sighed. If only that didn't seem like such a waste, she thought, not just of her degree, but of her passion for justice. No, she was simply meant to be a lawyer. She just had to rethink the way she practiced, which cases she accepted.

Satisfied that the third option wasn't really an option at all, she crossed it off the list.

That left one last possibility, at least for now. She could stay right here, open her own practice and be near her sisters. It would combine several advantages. She could have her fresh start, stay in law and still be close to family. The only negative was the prospect of running into Josh from time to time, but maybe he'd go back to his fancy Richmond law office any day now and never set foot in this region again.

If it turned out that he did pop up occasionally, she could live with that, she concluded thoughtfully. They were both adults. What was the big deal? They'd had an affair and it hadn't worked out. Happened all the time and people got over it and moved on. It didn't have to make her heart ache forever that he'd betrayed her and she'd apparently hurt him just as badly. She'd just have to chalk it up to bad timing, bad karma, something like that. She'd get over it. He would, too.

Tears pricked the back of her eyes, and she knew it was a lie. She wasn't going to get over it. Certainly not anytime soon. That meant she had to deal with it.

She ripped off the sheets of paper on which she'd listed her career options and wrote down another heading: *What to Do About Josh?*

The answers weren't half as clear-cut as she would have liked. Much as she hated to admit it, she needed another perspective. The prospect of going to Maggie and Melanie and telling them what a mess things had become held no appeal at all. Sooner or later, she would be forced to do it, but not this afternoon.

What she needed this afternoon was a distraction. She needed to mull things over, let her mind drift until the answers rose to the surface.

There was only one good way that she could think of to do that, since fishing with Josh was not a possibility. She hauled out the kayak and the new paddle she'd purchased. With any luck, a couple of hours of hard exercise would drive the whole Josh dilemma from her mind.

But the instant she put the kayak in the water, the memory of the first day she'd taken it out came flooding back to her. She pulled the paddle out of the water and let the tears she'd held back earlier come flooding out. They were hot and endless, proving that it wasn't going to be half as easy to put Josh behind her as she'd hoped.

Her tears eventually slowed to a sad trickle, and she was drifting when he pulled alongside her in his rowboat.

"Ashley?" There was an unmistakable note of worry in his voice.

She wanted to disappear. She didn't want him to know that he'd caused her one second of anguish. "Go away."

"Not with you floating around fifty feet from shore crying your eyes out. I could hear you from a hundred yards away."

Embarrassment turned her cheeks red. She'd had no idea she was sobbing so noisily. "I'm not crying over you," she said, feeling it vital not to let him think she was.

"Never thought you were," he said, though his lips quirked just a little.

"And I don't need you to rescue me."

"Of course not," he agreed. "I'll just stick close by, in case the waterworks get out of hand again and the kayak starts filling with water. Doesn't take much to swamp a little thing like that."

She finally lifted her gaze to meet his and wiped away the traces of tears on her cheeks. "Not going to happen," she said fiercely. "See, dry-eyed. You can go now."

He looked as if he wanted to say something more, but eventually he merely nodded. "Okay, then. I'll see you around."

She held on to the paddle until her knuckles turned white as she waited for him to disappear from view.

Oh, yeah, it was obvious she could handle bumping into him, she thought with self-derision. She'd all but come unglued just at the sound of his voice. A part of her had wanted to dive over into that rowboat so she could fling herself into his arms. Given that he was just as furious with her as she was with him, that could only have come to a bad end. It was entirely possible he'd have tossed her straight overboard. Just because he'd been worried finding her drifting along on the water didn't mean he was any more ready to forgive her than she was to forgive him. He would have done the same for anyone, because that's who he was…a nice guy.

Well, she didn't need his concern. Or his sympathy. Or his pity. In fact, the last would be unbearable.

Which meant she had to get over him. Right now. A nearly hysterical sob rose up. Sure, like she could snap her fingers and make that happen.

Much as she hated to admit it, she was probably way too much like her sisters. Once she gave away her heart, which she'd apparently done without giving it a conscious thought, it was all but impossible to take it back.

Josh hadn't wanted to feel a damn thing when he'd spotted Ashley out in that ridiculous kayak that she didn't know how to handle. He'd wanted to turn around and row away before she even knew he was around, but the instant he'd heard her sobs, his heart had flipped over. He hadn't been able to make himself leave, not without assuring himself that she would be okay. He figured his appearance alone would snap her out of it, and it had up to a point.

Making her mad had accomplished the rest well enough. He knew she'd hate his pity, so he'd done his best to act solicitous and sympathetic, knowing that she would place the worst possible spin on that and assume it was based on pity. What he'd wanted to do was to haul her into his boat and into his arms. That wasn't a good idea for either of them right now.

He figured he'd eventually get over his own hurt feelings, but first he had to understand how he'd allowed her opinion to matter so much. He had a feeling it went back to those days when he'd known she was out of reach and he'd felt inadequate.

This afternoon, for the first time since they'd met as adults, she'd made him feel inadequate all over again. To have that happen after being so close to her had ripped all of his hard-earned self-confidence apart. It was like discovering indescribable joy only to have it snatched away because he didn't measure up in some way that couldn't be changed.

He arrived back at Idylwild in time to hear the phone ringing. He managed to grab it before it stopped.

"Hello," he said breathlessly.

"Josh, I thought you were in better shape," Stephanie teased. "Or have I called at a bad time?"

"Very funny. What's up?"

"You're making my father very unhappy," she said. "And the worst of it is, he's blaming me."

"You? Why?"

"Because I won't bend to his will and come chasing after you," she said dryly. "He's sure we can work out all the pesky things bothering us and eventually find our way to the altar, after all."

"That just shows how stubborn he is," Josh said. "He's obviously not listening to either one of us. At least I assume you've told him the same thing I have, that we're not right for each other."

"I've tried," she said, "but you know my father. He ignores anything that doesn't agree with his view of the world."

"Then what do you suggest?"

"Come back to Richmond. We see him together and present a united front, so he can't dismiss this as some silly misunderstanding. Maybe then he'll get it and get off my case. Otherwise I'm afraid any other man I bring around will be doomed. Dad will only compare them to you and find them lacking."

Josh laughed. "Is there a compliment in there somewhere?"

"You are a tough act to follow, Josh. There's no question about it." She hesitated. "Did you need reminding of that for some reason?"

"As a matter of fact, I did," he said. "If it'll help you out, I'll come back to go with you to see your father." In that instant he made up his mind about something else that had been weighing on him. "But I have to warn you, Steph, I intend to quit while I'm there."

"Oh, jeez," she said with an exaggerated moan. "Can you at least wait till I get out of town?"

"Afraid not."

"Out of the room?"

"I can do that," he promised, smiling.

"What are your plans?" she asked him.

"I'm going to move down here and open up a practice," he said decisively. "It's what I should have done from the beginning. I'm not cut out for the barracuda pool."

"No, you're not," she agreed. "You have the talent, but not the bloodlust. That's one of the things I like most about you."

"I think that could be the nicest thing you've ever said to me," Josh told her.

"Oh, I'm sure I said a few more flattering things from time to time," she teased, then turned serious. "Are we okay, Josh? Can we go on being friends? I'd miss that a lot."

"Absolutely. You're the best one I have."

"Can I ask you something?"

"Anything."

"Is she worth it?"

His heart lurched. "Is who worth it?"

"Whoever you're moving down there to be with. There has to be a woman involved."

Josh sighed. He saw no point in denying it. "I thought she was."

"Has she done something to change your mind? Has she hurt you?" Stephanie demanded indignantly.

"Whoa, girl! You don't need to swoop down here to protect me."

"I will, you know."

"I know and I'm grateful."

"So are you sure this a good time for you to get away? I don't want to mess up whatever you have going on."

"Actually, your timing couldn't be better," he told her honestly. A day or two away might allow the dust to settle.

"Then when will you come down here to see my father?"

"Is tomorrow okay? We might as well get this over with."

"I'll set up lunch at the club," Stephanie told him. "He'll be much more mellow after a Scotch, a steak and a cigar."

"Mellow or dead," Josh said wryly. "He needs to quit all of those things."

"Which I've told him repeatedly, but since he hasn't, I intend to use them to my advantage," she said, sounding decidedly chipper. "See you tomorrow at noon."

Josh hung up, then went to stare out the same window where he'd found Ashley earlier. Had it only been that morning? He felt as if an eternity had gone by. He waited to see if he would catch a glimpse of her on the water, but she didn't appear.

He wondered how she would take the news that he was relocating, or if it would even matter to her. Probably not. He couldn't let her reaction matter to him, either. This was the right thing to do. He'd known it the minute he'd uttered the words to Stephanie. For the first time in months, he honestly felt as if his future were on the right track.

Now if only he had the right woman by his side.

Chapter Fourteen

When Josh stopped for coffee on his way out of town, he ran into Mike and Rick. He hesitated at the café door, but they spotted him before he could turn right around and leave. Reluctantly, he went to join them. He had a hunch they were going to want to get into things he had no intention of discussing.

"Going somewhere important?" Mike asked, noting the unaccustomed suit Josh was wearing.

"I have a meeting in Richmond," Josh admitted, figuring that was safe enough ground.

"Big case?" Rick asked.

"Nope, my boss and his daughter, the woman he expected me to marry."

Both men regarded him with amazement. "And you're walking into that willingly?"

"Eagerly, in fact," he told them. "Stephanie and I intend to convince her father that we would have made each other miserable, then I intend to quit my job. It's not going to be a great morning for Creighton Williams. He doesn't like being thwarted when he has things all planned out."

"Isn't he the lawyer who cuts the opposition into itty-bitty pieces at trial?" Mike asked worriedly.

"The very one."

"You're a braver man than I," Mike said.

"It has to be done," Josh told them. "Then I'll be free to come back here and open a practice."

"Does anyone else know about this?" Rick asked.

"If by anyone you mean Ashley, the answer is no. We're not exactly on speaking terms these days. This has nothing to do with her. It's a decision I should have made years ago, but I was blinded by dollar signs."

"Mind if I ask why you think this doesn't affect Ashley?" Mike inquired.

Josh regarded him with surprise. "You don't know?"

"Not me," Mike said. He turned to Rick. "You?"

"Haven't heard a word," Rick confirmed.

Josh wasn't sure what to make of that. He'd been sure Ashley would run to her sisters with the tale of how he'd betrayed her. Maybe she'd been too embarrassed that she'd missed something so obvious about the man she was sleeping with.

"Bottom line, she found out I was a lawyer before I could tell her." He gave them a rueful smile. "You underestimated her fury. Then I discovered that she'd assumed I did some sort of menial, undemanding labor and that it suited her just fine, because that made me safe, since she couldn't possibly fall in love with someone with so little ambition."

"Safe and unambitious?" Mike said, his expression puzzled. He glanced at Rick, then back toward Josh. "Is that as demeaning as it sounds?"

"I certainly thought it was," Josh said. "Things pretty much went downhill from there."

"Yet you're coming back here to go into practice," Rick said. "Why?"

"Because it will give me the chance to practice the kind of law I always wanted to practice, helping regular folks with the things that matter to them, instead of big corporations that only want to get bigger."

"And you honestly don't see Ashley anywhere in this picture?" Mike asked.

Josh hesitated. He didn't want to admit just how badly he wanted her to be a part of it, not after what had happened between them. What would it say about him that he was willing to grovel to make it happen? Bottom line, though, she had to discover on her own exactly how well-suited they were and that they could be professional as well as emotional partners.

"You can admit it, pal," Rick teased eventually. "We won't think any less of you. We've both been there. The D'Angelo women are worth whatever it takes to keep them."

Josh was surprised by Rick's understanding. "You don't think I'm an idiot for wanting her, even after she proved how little respect she had for me?"

"Personally, I think you're looking at it all wrong," Mike said. "I think it's a testament to how much she respected you that she overlooked what she was sure were your shortcomings and fell in love with you anyway."

It was an interesting spin, but that's all it was. Even so, Josh desperately wanted to believe him. "You think so?"

Rick grinned. "If that's the interpretation that gets you through this impasse, then hang on to it for dear life. Pride's a mighty cold bedfellow."

Josh nodded slowly. "I'll keep that in mind. Now I'd better hit the road, so I can get this over with. I can't have much of a future, if I don't deal with the past once and for all."

"Good luck," they both told him as he scooted out of the booth.

"Thanks." He wasn't going to need it, though. It was an image of the prize at the end of it all—the albeit slim possibility of a future with Ashley—that was going to get him through today.

"Are you seeing the big picture here?" Maggie asked when Ashley told her the whole story about discovering that Josh was an attorney with a firm in Richmond that was so influential she'd heard about it all the way in Boston.

"He lied to me," Ashley said flatly. She didn't want to hear her sister's spin on that. The lying was the only thing that mattered. "How can trust flourish when one person lies about something so basic? And without trust, what kind of relationship can we possibly have?"

"Maybe it was a lie. Maybe not," Maggie said anyway. "Josh said he was here to think about what he wants, the same as you have been. Haven't you wrestled with that on your own without asking for his input?"

"I suppose, but that hasn't stopped him from giving it to me," Ashley grumbled.

"But my point is," Maggie continued as if Ashley hadn't said a word, "this just gives you something more in common besides the great sex."

"Who said the sex was great?" Ashley retorted irritably.

"You did. Besides, if it wasn't, you wouldn't be so rattled by all of this," her sister said confidently. "You'd write him off, finish making up your mind about what you want to do for the rest of your life and then get on with it. Have you thought about that, by the way? Or has the issue that brought you running down here taken a back seat to your feelings for Josh? If so, what does that say about your priorities these days?"

The truth was she hadn't thought about anything except Josh for days now. Since everyone around her knew it, she might as well admit it. "No," she responded testily. "My priorities have gotten a little confused. That's all the more reason to forget about Josh and get back to what's important."

"There is nothing more important than love," Maggie said. "A very wise older sister once told me that."

"Must have been someone else," Ashley insisted sourly.

"Come on, Ashley, admit it," Maggie chided. "Doesn't it tell you something that your priorities have changed since you came here? You've actually found someone who's more important to you than work."

"He's not," Ashley said fiercely. "I won't let him be."

Maggie laughed. "Too late, sweetie. You don't get to control everything, you know. Some things just are. Love is one of them."

"I will not be in love with Josh." She said it with more wistfulness than conviction. Naturally her sister picked right up on that.

"Good luck with that one," Maggie replied. "Keep me posted."

Ashley scowled at her. "I can still go back to Boston. In fact, that was exactly what I intended to do as soon as I talked to Josh night before last. Then one thing sort of led to another, I wound up spending the night there and then yesterday morning I stumbled across this little bombshell."

"Why did you come here today?" Maggie asked. "Why didn't you just leave for Boston? What's keeping you here?"

"I wish to hell I knew." She gave Maggie a bemused look. "God, I hate this uncertainty. I used to know how to make quick, clean decisions and live with the consequences."

Maggie laughed. "Tell me something I don't know about you." She gave Ashley a penetrating look. "Why are you confused? Seems to me if you're really through with Josh, if you really think he's a pig, then there's no reason to stick around."

"Logically, you're right," Ashley admitted.

"But logic has nothing to do with it, sweetie. Josh suddenly seems more suitable, now that you know he's a lawyer, doesn't he?"

"Yes," she admitted. "That's part of it."

"Do you realize just how shallow that sounds?"

"Yes," she said miserably. "Believe me, he called me on it, too."

"You still haven't answered my question. Do you

want to go back to Boston as much right now as you did when you first found out? Or do you want to stay and fight for what you could have with a good, decent guy who happens to love you?"

"I like it here," she admitted, still a little stunned by that fact. Even in the throes of discovering that Josh had lied to her, she'd realized how much she would miss him and Rose Cottage. That realization had changed everything. In fact, it had left her torn. It had ruined the cold logic she usually used when analyzing her lists.

"Then stay," Maggie said as if the decision were easy.

"It's not that simple. I like being here with Josh, and maybe we could get past this monumental lie or omission or whatever, but Josh doesn't live here, or have you forgotten that?"

"I haven't forgotten anything," Maggie said calmly. "Not even the fact that D'Angelo women fight the hardest when they're about to go down for the count."

Rick wandered in just then and overheard them. "Guess you haven't heard," he said, picking up an apple and biting into it.

"Heard what?" Maggie prodded.

"Josh is gone."

Ashley felt her heart tumble straight to her toes. "He's gone? Where? Back to Richmond?"

"Uh-huh. I spoke to him this morning right before he took off."

"I see," Ashley said, her voice flat. It really was over then. He hadn't stuck around to fight for her. That hurt a hell of a lot more than she'd expected it to.

"Not sure you do," Rick said, a surprising twinkle in his eyes.

Maggie gave him an impatient look. "If you have something to say, spit it out. This is not the time for games."

He looked unrepentant. "I thought maybe it was. Seems to me that your sister's reaction was very telling." He turned to Ashley. "You felt as if the wind had been knocked out of you, didn't you?"

She stared at him with a narrowed gaze. "Your point?"

"That you're in love with the man."

"Well, of course, she is," Maggie said.

"I am not," Ashley said, but without much conviction. "Okay, of course I am. Admitting that does me a fat lot of good when he's gone back to Richmond."

"You could go after him," Rick suggested, then added slyly, "Or you could wait till he gets back tomorrow."

The sudden pounding of Ashley's heart told her everything she needed to know. "He's coming back?" she asked, trying to keep the hope out of her voice. It was humiliating how badly she wanted to have another chance.

Rick nodded. "He went down there to quit his job. He's decided this is where he wants to live."

Maggie scowled at him. "And why did he confide all this to you, rather than Ashley?"

"Because we were there," Rick said simply. "Besides, the way I hear it, they aren't speaking."

"Where?" Ashley asked, ignoring the comment about the lack of communication between her and Josh at the moment.

"At the café. He had breakfast this morning with Mike and me."

"And he thought you should be the first to know about this important, life-altering decision? Guess that shows where I fit in," Ashley said.

"Hey," Rick protested. "I thought you women were all in favor of us bonding with him and pumping him for information."

"You're supposed to share it," Maggie reminded him impatiently.

He stared at her. "I just did. Was I supposed to call on my cell phone from the café? You know the damn thing never works."

"Okay, you two," Ashley scolded. "Play nice. I won't have you fighting because of me and my problems."

"Sounds to me like you don't have any problems," Maggie said, suddenly more cheerful. "Josh is coming back. You can make things right with him, if that's what you want. Is it?"

"He's furious with me, too," she reminded her sister. "He might not want to make things right." She glanced at Rick, to see if he'd admit to any insights on this point, but he was suddenly silent.

"Oh, no," Maggie scoffed. "He's just giving up his thriving law practice with a prestigious Richmond firm so he can be near the water."

"Actually, that's exactly it," Rick said.

Maggie frowned at him. "You're not helping."

Ashley turned to Rick. "It has nothing at all to do with me?"

"How could it? He doesn't know what you intend to do."

Her spirits sank. "I see."

Maggie gave her a hard hug. "Stop it. You look as if

it's over. It's not. You have a second chance. You just have to grab it the minute he gets back to town."

Ashley nodded slowly. Her pride was screaming that Josh ought to make the first move. She'd try to tell her pride to shut up and be reasonable, but the reality was that she usually let it rule her decisions. Wasn't it pride that had made her scurry out of Boston just when she should have stayed there with her head held high? Her uncharacteristic retreat had probably only fueled the media frenzy she'd left in her wake.

She made a decision of her own then. "I have something I need to do," she told Maggie and Rick, gathering up her purse and the jacket she'd worn over.

"What?" Maggie asked.

"I'm going home."

"Home?"

She nodded. "To Boston. There are some things I need to take care of."

Her sister's gaze narrowed. "But you'll be back?"

"In a few days."

Rick looked completely confused. "What should I tell Josh if he asks?"

Ashley and Maggie both turned to him at once. "Stay out of it!" they said in a chorus.

He frowned at both of them. "Is it any wonder men don't understand women? You keep changing the blasted rules on us."

Ashley gave her brother-in-law a kiss on the cheek. "Stick around, pal. You'll get the hang of it eventually. I can see your potential. Obviously Maggie can, too, or she wouldn't have married you."

"Small consolation," he grumbled, but he pulled

Maggie into his arms and kissed her so thoroughly it made Ashley's mouth go dry.

"I'm out of here," she said hurriedly.

She was pretty sure neither one of them heard her or even gave a damn.

The meeting with Creighton went off with surprisingly few hitches, Josh concluded after the lunch ended. Oh, the man had grumbled and carried on about Josh being ungrateful and shortsighted, but in the end it was obvious that he wanted his daughter to be happy and he respected Josh enough to accept the decision he had made, as well. They had parted on good terms, with the door at the firm always open if Josh woke up one morning and realized he'd made a tragic mistake, which Creighton direly predicted Josh would most certainly do.

Josh was so eager to get back and find Ashley that he decided against staying over in Richmond for the night to put his condo on the market, and drove straight back down to Idylwild instead. Rick and Mike had been right. He couldn't allow this misunderstanding to fester until it turned into something insurmountable. He had to be the one to hold out an olive branch.

But when he arrived around dinnertime, he couldn't find Ashley at Rose Cottage or anywhere else in town. Finally, as a last resort, he drove out to Maggie's. When she answered the door, she gave him a hard look.

"Yes?" she said in a tone that would have made him quake if he hadn't seen the twinkle in her eyes.

"I'm looking for Ashley."

"You're too late."

His heart fell. "Too late?"

"She went back to Boston."

Josh felt as if someone had punched him in the stomach. "I see."

Maggie shook her head and regarded him with pity. "You'd better come in. I can't have you passing out on my doorstep. Ashley would never forgive me."

"I'm not going to pass out," he said with more spirit.

"Come in, anyway. Based on your unmistakable reaction to the news, we probably need to talk."

He frowned at the determined note in her voice. He didn't trust that tone one bit. "Again?"

She laughed. "Oh, don't whine, Josh. I'll make it relatively painless."

"You might as well do it," Rick called out. "Otherwise she'll just have to hunt you down. Believe me, persistence is one of her best traits. Sticking around now will save time in the long run."

Josh focused on Rick as he stepped inside. "Thank goodness," he muttered. "A friendly face."

"Don't rely on my husband to save you," Maggie warned. "I want to know what your intentions are toward my sister and I want to know now. And just to give you a fair heads-up, they'd better be honorable."

Josh gave her an amused look. "Isn't that a little old-fashioned?"

"What can I say?" she said, not backing down. "I'm an old-fashioned girl. And in the absence of my father, it's my duty to get a few things straight with you." She gave him another of those hard looks. "Or, if you prefer, I can call him and drag him down here first thing in the morning. He's chewed up and spit out men like you every day since we hit sixteen."

Josh glanced at Rick, who was clearly getting entirely too much enjoyment out of the whole scene. "You could help, you know."

Rick shook his head. "Sorry, pal. You're on your own with this one. Maggie's a reasonable woman."

She beamed at him. "Thank you."

"Just being honest," Rick assured her. He grinned at Josh. "Tell the truth and you have nothing to fear."

Josh shot a sour look in his direction, then turned it on Maggie. "I repeat, isn't this a conversation I should be having with Ashley?"

Maggie returned his look with a perfectly bland expression. "That depends," she said sweetly. "She's not here at the moment. I am. And, trust me, you won't ever get close enough to talk to her unless I like what I hear."

Josh shook his head. "Then I'd say we're at an impasse, because I don't intend to discuss this with you. Suffice it to say that it is not my intention to hurt your sister."

"You already have," she reminded him.

"Not deliberately," he replied. "And she didn't exactly make me feel all fluttery and special. She thought I was a fisherman."

"There's nothing wrong with fishing for a living," Maggie said. "It's a perfectly respectable profession, especially around here."

"I agree, but it was plain that your sister didn't see it in such a positive light. She acted as if she'd been doing me a damn favor by condescending to sleep with me when I had nothing at all to offer her." The bitterness welled up again as he spoke. He hated that their relationship had begun with lies, evasions and misunderstandings, but it was too late to change that. They had to deal with who they really were and the undeniable attraction that couldn't be dismissed just because of hurt feelings.

Maggie regarded him with surprising compassion. "I'm sorry. You have no idea how terrible she feels about that. Ashley isn't a snob. If anything, she was just trying to protect herself from emotions that were too huge for her to accept."

"Small comfort," Josh said. Ironically, even as he spoke with such sarcasm, he realized it was true. It was some comfort to know that she'd been in deeper than she'd expected to be and had latched on to any excuse for an escape.

"She loves you," Maggie said more gently. "She really does."

He met her sympathetic gaze and finally found the courage to admit what he hadn't said to anyone else, including himself. "I love her, too."

A grin filled with unmistakable relief spread across Maggie's face. "There now," she said, patting his arm. "That wasn't so difficult, was it?"

He couldn't help grinning at her obvious sense of triumph. "No worse than a tooth extraction," he retorted. "Now may I please go?"

"Where? Boston?"

"Absolutely not," he said at once. "If this is going to work, it has to work here. She has to come back on her own." He studied Maggie intently. "Think she will?"

"Not a doubt in my mind."

Josh nodded. He was counting on the fact that no one knew the D'Angelo sisters any better than they knew each other.

Chapter Fifteen

Ashley stood in front of a bank of television and radio microphones and drew in a deep breath. This was it. This was what she should have had the courage to do weeks ago. She was going to face the people of Boston and the family of Letitia Baldwin and admit that she had lost sight of the promise she had made to herself when she first went into law…to focus on justice, not winning. Perhaps it simply wasn't practical to believe that every client she defended would be innocent, but she had intended to do her very best not to fall prey to the cynicism that afflicted too many criminal defense attorneys.

"Good morning, ladies and gentlemen," she said at last, proud that neither her gaze, nor her voice faltered, not even when she spotted her parents and Jo in the back of the room. Her sister gave her a broad smile and a thumbs-up gesture.

"Thank you for coming. I have a brief prepared statement and then I'll take a few of the questions I'm certain you've stored up in my absence."

The last drew a laugh from some of the veteran reporters at the front of the pack. They all knew that she'd never before been reticent with the media. In fact, she'd always enjoyed a lively give-and-take with most of them. Her silence since that awful day in the courtroom had spoken volumes. It had conveyed her sense of shame and guilt, emotions she had to put behind her if she was ever to function effectively in a courtroom again.

She glanced at the cameramen to be sure they were set up. "Shall we get started?" At their nods, she looked directly into the closest camera. "Although I have done so privately, I would like to publicly apologize to Letitia Baldwin's family, as well as to the people of this city for the part I played in the miscarriage of justice that occurred in Tiny Slocum's trial. I could tell you that I was just doing my job and that would be true, but it's a sad truth when a guilty man goes free because of it. I could tell you that I believed in Tiny Slocum's innocence and that would be true as well, but it doesn't say much about my judgment, and for that I am deeply sorry."

Her chin rose a notch. "I know that I can't change any of that, but I can promise you and, just as importantly, myself, that I will never again go into a case without evaluating the impact of my defense more thoroughly and being absolutely certain in my heart that what I'm doing serves the cause of justice. I owe that much to the honor of this profession."

She swallowed hard and fought to hold her gaze steady. "Now I'll take those questions."

"Ms. D'Angelo, will you continue to practice law?" Lynda Stone, daytime anchor for a network affiliate, asked. "And why haven't you been around to answer questions?"

They'd never gotten along and it seemed to Ashley as if the woman was eager to gloat over Ashley's current professional predicament. Ashley met her gaze evenly. "Let me answer the last question first. I needed some time to think about what had happened and my role in it. As for your other question, absolutely, I will continue to practice law, though I'll admit to having had a lot of self-doubts in recent weeks. In the end, I realized that I still believe passionately in our legal system. Nothing is perfect, but it's the best one on the face of the earth. And I think I can still make a valuable contribution."

"Really?" Ms. Stone asked, her voice laced with skepticism. "You honestly think you can be effective after this? Will any jury trust you?"

"One case, one mistake, doesn't negate a track record like mine," Ashley said succinctly. "And cases should be won or lost based on the evidence, not the attorneys involved. In the end, that's what happened in this one. Sadly, the prosecutor didn't come into the case fully prepared with indisputable evidence. I'll leave it to others to decide if the fault was his or the police department's. Unfortunately as it turned out, I was able to take advantage of that in defense of my client."

"Would you conduct the defense the same way if you had to do it over?" the anchorwoman asked.

"If you're asking if I'd defend Mr. Slocum in the same way knowing he was guilty, the answer is no. I would have done everything in my power to persuade him to accept a plea bargain."

"And if he had refused?" Ms. Stone asked.

"I would have stepped down as his counsel," she said.

"Even though he's entitled to the best defense available?" Ms. Stone persisted.

Ashley nodded. "Yes. I have to live with my conscience. Besides, Boston has plenty of qualified criminal defense attorneys who could have handled his case, including others at my own firm."

"Very noble, now that you have the advantage of hindsight," the anchorwoman said bitingly. "Will you stay with that firm?"

Ashley was certain from the malicious glint in the woman's eyes that she already knew the answer. "I believe some of you already know that I've quit."

"Why is that?" The question came from an unfamiliar reporter in the back of the room.

"I no longer felt we were a good fit. I'm sure the partners agreed," she said wryly. "But, of course, I wouldn't dream of speaking for them."

"Even though they had no problem speaking for you?" Frank Lyman asked. "In fact, they seemed quite eager to jump into the spotlight."

Ashley had always found Frank's biting wit a breath of fresh air. It was so again this morning. "Some people abhor a vacuum," she commented. "And if there was one in this instance, I created it by running away. I'm sure they felt they had to fill the void."

"You're being very gracious," someone commented. "Don't you feel as if they were capitalizing on a tragedy?"

"I'll leave it to you to interpret their motives."

Lynda Stone gave her another smirking look. "Any other firms in town made an offer to you?"

Ashley refused to lose her cool. "None knew until this moment that I might be available, but thank you for giving me an opportunity to put the word out." She smiled. "Unfortunately, though, my plan is to go into private practice elsewhere."

"Where?" the woman prodded. "New York? Washington?"

Ashley saw what she was trying to do. Unless Ashley came up with some dream offer, anything else Ashley said would sound like a demotion of sorts, a step down. She gave her reply careful thought. She refused to let anyone think she was running away because she thought she couldn't cut it in the big leagues anymore.

"I've had a few weeks to sort out my priorities," she began slowly. "I've found that not everything begins and ends in Boston. There are plenty of places in need of a lawyer with my skills and much satisfaction to be had in making sure that everyone has an equal shot at justice. I've also realized that there's more to life than the law and I hope to have an announcement on that front in the very near future."

Determined to end the press conference on her own terms, she beamed directly at Lynda Stone. "Thanks so much for giving me this opportunity to speak out. I'm sure we'll cross paths again."

She turned and walked away, this time with her shoulders back and her head held high. For the first time in weeks she felt as if she'd reclaimed her self-respect. As her parents and Jo came up to flank her, she realized it felt damn good.

Now it was time to get back to Virginia and fight for the man she loved.

Damn, but she was magnificent! Josh caught a snippet of Ashley's press conference on the national news. The miscarriage of justice in the Tiny Slocum case had made the network newscast a few weeks back. Because the attorney involved had been all but invisible, he hadn't realized at the time that it was Ashley. In fact, he hadn't put it all together until she'd told him about the dilemma that had brought her to Rose Cottage. Now he had to give the network credit for following up with Ashley's side of the story, albeit they gave her time for little more than a footnote compared to the length of the original segment.

He had a hunch offers would pour in once the other major law firms in Boston caught wind of the fact that a high-profile, talented lawyer was without a job. Any sensible firm would want such a class act with her incredible legal mind on staff. What would she do once they started dangling money and power in front of her? He wished he were convinced that she would choose Virginia, would choose *him*.

He couldn't sit around Idylwild waiting for her to come back, though. He'd go stir-crazy. He had decisions of his own to make, office space to lease, letterhead to be designed and printed. He had to go back to Richmond and put his condo on the market, pack up the few things that really mattered to him and sell the rest. None of that was contingent on Ashley's return.

But for some reason, he couldn't make himself get started. He wanted to know if they were going to be a team. More than that, he needed to know if she'd forgiven him, if she was even remotely interested in marrying a man who had a hefty bank account and a professional job.

He was still staring listlessly at the now-dark television screen when Mike appeared in the doorway. He'd gotten in the habit of strolling over whenever he was at loose ends. This visit had to mean that Melanie had taken Jessie somewhere for the day and left Mike to his own devices. It was almost pathetic how lost the man was without his wife and daughter. Josh was beginning to understand how he felt. He felt a little lost and vulnerable himself these days,

"You look like hell," Mike observed cheerfully.

"It's a good thing you're not hoping to pursue a career as a motivational speaker," Josh retorted.

"Want to go out for a beer?"

"No."

"Want to order a pizza?"

"No."

"I'm sensing a pattern here," Mike commented. "Are you up for company?"

"Not really." He regarded Mike speculatively. "I don't suppose you know if or when Ashley's coming back?"

"Sorry. I'm not in the loop on that one. Melanie's been walking around all grim-faced ever since that press conference on TV. She saw maybe ten seconds and concluded that the world is out to destroy her sister. I pity Lynda Stone if they ever cross paths. I'm not sure I realized my wife had such a vicious streak in her."

Josh stared at him in surprise. "Did Melanie see the same clip I saw? I thought Ashley was amazing."

Mike grinned. "You'd think she was amazing if she drew little stick figures and called it art."

"Possibly," he admitted.

"I assume, though, that seeing her on TV is what put you in this odd mood," Mike said.

He nodded.

"Why?" Mike asked.

"What if she decides she has to stay up there and fight for her reputation?"

Mike gave him a bland look. "What if she does?"

"How the hell will we work things out then?"

"Creatively," Mike said. "Planes fly. The phones around here work. You'll manage, at least if you want to badly enough." He gave him a sly look. "Or you could move to Boston."

Josh shuddered. "Not likely."

"You would if you loved her enough and it was where she had to be."

Would he do that in the name of love? Josh tried to imagine it and couldn't. Unfortunately, he couldn't envision his life anywhere without Ashley in it. He supposed if that meant moving to Boston, he'd find a way to handle it. He'd played in a shark-infested pool before. He could do it again, especially with Ashley added to the stakes.

In the meantime, though, maybe he'd take a leap of faith and put a deposit down on office space right here in town. With luck, he'd find a place with room enough for two lawyers just in case she decided to come back and they worked things out.

He got to his feet, grabbed a jacket and headed for the door.

Mike stared after him without budging. "Where are you going?"

"To put a down payment on my future," he said at once. "Want to come?"

Mike grinned. "Can I call Melanie first?"

"Absolutely not."

Mike seemed to weigh that for a minute, then shrugged. "Oh, well. How much hell can she put me through? Count me in."

Ashley had been back in town for twenty-four hours and she still hadn't seen Josh. She'd debated simply calling him, but each time she'd reached for the phone, she'd stopped herself. She'd done a lot of thinking in Boston and she knew what she wanted. At least she thought she did.

She did know that they needed to have this conversation in person. She wanted to look into his eyes when she told him she was staying. She needed to see if that mattered to him at all.

Half a dozen times she was tempted to take her kayak out on the water and paddle along until she ran into him, hopefully not literally again. But she had too much pride to do it. Besides, it was cold as hell out and he was the one who owed her an apology, at least almost as much as she owed him one. She had to give him time to reach that conclusion on his own. If he didn't, well, she could still take matters into her own hands. She wouldn't let this absurd impasse go on forever.

Maybe the delay was a good thing. Maybe she

could manage to think clearly about what she really wanted without getting her hormones all tangled up in the decision. In Boston, she'd all but made up her mind to open a practice right here, but was it what she really wanted? Or had it been a knee-jerk reaction after she'd accepted that there was nothing left for her back home?

And how much of her thinking had been based on having a future with Josh? Could she stay here in this quiet place, maybe go into private practice, if Josh were never to be a part of her life?

She sat beside her kitchen window looking out at the brilliant blue sky, the calm water reflecting the trees that had already turned, their leaves now bright splashes of autumn colors. She felt the once-familiar calm steal through her. How long had it been since she'd known such a blissful lack of stress? Years, if she were being totally honest about it. She'd thought she needed the stress to survive, but she didn't. She'd discovered that other things made her feel alive.

Yes, she could stay. In fact, she was eager to stay. She'd tapped into a serenity here that she'd never expected to want or enjoy. Now she knew she needed it to be a whole woman and not just a workaholic lawyer.

And she had family here. Maggie and Melanie were building their lives here. Boston would always be home, but with her parents and Jo still there, she could visit as often as she wanted to. Maybe this place was even in her soul, just as it was in her mother's. Maybe there was something to this whole roots business that made her feel as if she'd *come* home, rather than run away from it.

She glanced around Rose Cottage and considered

the whimsical notion that it was magical. Maybe it was. Two of her sisters had fallen in love here. There was no denying that. Now she was on the same path.

"I want to stay," she said aloud, testing the words, testing the sentiment. The instant she'd said it, the last of the second thoughts faded and she felt an even deeper kind of peace steal through her.

An hour later she was standing in front of a building with office space for rent in Irvington. Real estate wasn't exactly easy to come by now that the area had been discovered by other professionals looking for a more leisurely way of life.

"Sorry I'm late, but my other appointment took longer than I expected. I have to tell you that someone else is interested in this space, too," the real estate agent said when she finally arrived looking harried. "He looked at it an hour ago."

Ashley seized on what the woman hadn't said. "But he didn't put down a deposit?"

"No. He had to go home for his checkbook. I probably shouldn't even be showing it to you, since he said he'd be back any minute now, but I've had enough be-back customers in my day to know to hedge my bets. I want to be honest with you, though. If he does show up, he has first crack at it."

Ashley slipped into full-lawyer mode. Even without going inside, she could tell this space would be perfect. It was on a main street in a Victorian house that had been converted to offices. The available space was on the first floor with windows facing the street and the giant oak tree that shaded the porch. The building had history, substance and charm. She was ready to fight for it. "Did he sign any papers? Did you make a verbal agreement to hold it?"

The woman looked at her curiously. "Let me guess. You're a lawyer."

Ashley gave her a rueful nod. "I guess it shows."

"Funny. It showed on him, too." Her eyes lit speculatively. "It's a big space. If you hit if off, maybe you could hook up, go into practice together."

"I don't think so," Ashley said, but the words trailed off when she spotted Josh pulling into a parking space right beside them.

"Is that the other prospective tenant?" she asked the woman.

"Oh, my," she said worriedly. "It is. I hope he's not furious about this."

"Let me handle it," Ashley said, then snatched a dollar out of her pocket. "There's my deposit. You'll get the rest in ten minutes."

"But you haven't even seen it."

"Doesn't matter," Ashley said. "It will do. Now I have another negotiation to complete. Meet me inside in ten minutes."

The agent glanced from Josh to her and back again. "If you say so."

He looked so good. Better than he had a right to. He should have looked as miserable as she had felt every minute since they'd fought. He stood where he was, regarding her suspiciously.

"What are you doing here?" he asked.

"Same thing you are, apparently. Trying to rent office space."

An unmistakable spark of hope lit in his eyes. "Really?"

She nodded, her gaze locked on his face. "I'm staying, Josh. You'll just have to get used to it."

"So am I," he said easily. "Think you can get used to that?" There was an undeniable challenge in his voice.

She nodded confidently. "I know I can. In fact, I was counting on it."

Silence fell. It lasted for what seemed like an eternity before he finally spoke again.

"Think we can get past the mistakes we both made?" he asked. "You were awfully furious with me."

"Are you reminding me of how angry I was just so I'll give up and let you have this office?"

"I'm reminding you because I need to know that's in the past. I'm reminding you because I love you and I hate being separated from you. I want you to be sure, because it would kill me if you walked away again."

She barely contained a sigh of relief. "I have an idea," she said, kicking pride out of the window to reach for what she wanted, what she needed. "Want to rent part of that space from me? I'll negotiate a fair deal."

He grinned. "Nice try, but that space is mine. I might consider letting you share it."

She gave him a wicked grin of her own. "I'm the one who put a deposit down, smart guy."

"But I had a verbal agreement with the agent. I can sue to make sure she honors it."

"You could," Ashley admitted.

"Then, again, I think I might have a better idea."

"Oh?"

"We could get married and share a life that just happens to include this office space."

Why quibble over terms, when it was the deal

she'd been praying for? She held out her hand. "Deal."

"Just like that?" he asked, looking vaguely surprised.

"I'm going to trust my judgment on this one. I don't think it's letting me down, after all."

"I won't let you down, that's for sure. Not if I can help it."

Instead of taking her hand, he pulled her into his arms and kissed her thoroughly. "Now we have a deal," he said firmly. "We'll seal it in a church with all the appropriate bells and whistles, but it's binding now."

"Spoken like a true lawyer," she said, oddly pleased. It was something she would have said herself, if he'd given her the chance.

"You're not still furious that I don't fish for a living?"

She shook her head. "Not as long as you take me with you from time to time when we play hooky from the office."

"That's a promise."

"And you'll bait my hook," she said, going for broke as long as he was in such an amenable mood.

He laughed. "You can bait your own hook, sweetheart. In fact, I should probably have you bait mine. You've reeled in more fish lately than I have."

She wound her arms around his neck. "Reeled myself in a big one just this afternoon, in fact."

Ashley glanced up just then and saw the real estate agent staring down at them with a stunned expression.

"We'll take it," she called up.

A grin spread over the woman's face.

"What made you say yes so quickly?" Ashley asked Josh. "I know I'd hurt you."

He shrugged. "Maybe I saw you slip her that dollar and this was the only way I could think of to make sure my law practice didn't wind up homeless."

"You'd marry me just to have a decent law office?" she inquired with a hint of indignation.

"No, I'd marry you under any condition. The office is just a nice bonus," he assured her.

"How will I ever know that for sure?"

"To prove how much I love and respect you, I'll let you put your name first on the door. How about that?"

"D'Angelo and Madison? Sounds good to me."

He shook his head. "Madison and Madison sounds even better."

Ashley laughed. "You really are a clever lawyer, aren't you?"

"Takes one to know one, darlin'."

Epilogue

"I am getting very tired of my daughters getting married in such a hurry that there's no time to plan a proper wedding," Colleen D'Angelo said wearily as the entire family relaxed in the parlor of the family home in Boston after Ashley and Josh's wedding ceremony.

The guests had gone, but Ashley and Josh were still there. He'd insisted on going over the marriage license one last time to make sure every *t* had been crossed and every *i* had been dotted. Ashley could have told him they had been because she'd gone over it herself, several times, in fact.

She slipped her arms around his waist. "You know that piece of paper isn't what really matters," she told him.

"Then why'd we go through all this fuss that obviously wore your mother out just to get it?"

"Because living in sin wasn't in the cards. In this family, we do things the old-fashioned way."

He turned and pressed a kiss to her lips. "You don't strike me as an old-fashioned woman, Mrs. Madison. Are you going to stay home with the kids and bake cookies?"

"Nope," she said complacently. "I'm going to bring them with me to the office and pick up cookies from the bakery on the way. I think they'll get over the trauma of it."

He laughed. "I imagine they will." He studied her intently. "We never talked about kids. Maybe we should have. How many do you want?"

"Two, three. How about you?"

"I'm rather partial to four. I like the way you and your sisters stick together. I want our kids to have that."

"That doesn't have anything to do with the fact that there are four of us. It has to do with the way we were raised. Loyalty was ingrained in us."

"I know." He glanced over at Jo. "What will happen to Jo now that the rest of you are going to be in Virginia? Won't she be a little lost?"

Ashley had worried about the very same thing. She'd even tried discussing it with Jo, but her baby sister had insisted she was going to be just fine in Boston. Unspoken was the fact that Jo had always kept herself a little apart from the rest of them.

"She says she's content here," Ashley said.

"I suppose she can always come and visit," Josh suggested.

"I said the same thing, but she had the oddest reaction. She brushed me off. She said she wasn't like the rest of us, that she had no intention of running away to Rose Cottage, not ever, no matter what happened in her life."

Rick looked as perplexed by that as Ashley had been. "I suppose there's no law that she has to like it down there, just because you, Melanie and Maggie do," he said.

"But that's just it," Ashley protested. "She always loved it as much as we did when we were kids. In fact, she could hardly wait to get back there each summer."

"Things change," Josh said. "She's an adult now."

"I still think it's weird. A couple of times when she drove down with us, she acted almost as if she didn't want to go out in public, as if she was afraid of something."

Josh's gaze turned speculative. "Or someone."

Ashley stared at him, her indignation immediately rising. "Do you think someone there hurt her?"

Josh grinned. "Slow down, tiger. I'm merely speculating. And to tell you the truth, I think there are a lot more interesting things we could be doing on our wedding night than worrying about your baby sister and manufacturing problems where there might not be any at all."

Ashley immediately responded to the heat in his eyes. "Think so?"

"Know so," he said. "I know this cozy little gathering is all for us, but I say it's time to head for our hotel room. We can get a head start on our honeymoon."

She laughed. "I think we've been getting a head start on that for weeks now. Where are we going, by the way? You still haven't told me."

"Because it's a surprise."

"I hate surprises."

He grinned. "I know, my darling control freak, but you'll love this one. Trust me."

She sighed and pressed her forehead to his, surrendering. "I do," she said softly. Despite everything that had happened to her, despite the betrayals she'd suffered, she did trust this man with her heart.

That didn't mean she didn't want to know where they were going first thing in the morning, though. "How am I supposed to pack?" she groused.

"Maggie packed for you," he assured her, his eyes glinting with amusement. "Besides, it's a honeymoon. How much clothing could you possibly need?"

"A lot more than you're obviously anticipating," she said, "especially if you keep playing games with me."

"I've got it covered," he insisted. "I promise."

"Is it warm? Cold?"

"There will be heat," he said cheerfully.

"Indoors or out?"

"Wherever we are," he assured her.

"You're really not going to tell me, are you?"

"No."

"Why?"

"Because it's a man's job to plan the honeymoon."

"Who says?"

"I read it somewhere."

She laughed at that. "You have not been reading books on wedding etiquette."

"I needed something to put me to sleep during all those lonely nights you were up here planning the wedding."

"I was gone for a week."

"Too long," he insisted. "One night is too long."

She smiled. "Then isn't it lucky that we're going to be together for the rest of our lives?"

"Damn straight," he said, waving the marriage license under her nose. "I made sure of it."

"No loopholes?" she teased.

"Not a one. This thing is airtight. Not even a lawyer as clever as you could find a loophole."

"Good," she said, pleased. "Because I intend to hold you to it."

Josh laughed. "Never doubted it for a minute."

* * * * *

And now, turn the page for a sneak preview of Jo D'Angelo's story,

FOR THE LOVE OF PETE,

the fourth book in Sherryl Woods's exciting new series,
ROSE COTTAGE SISTERS

On sale in June 2005 from Silhouette Special Edition.

Chapter One

As if to prove her sisters' point, snow had started falling an hour after Jo's arrival at Rose Cottage. She stared out the window as the big, wet flakes landed on the ground. With some effort, she bit back a hysterical sob.

"What?" Ashley asked, coming up to slide a comforting arm around her shoulders.

Jo turned to her big sister, her eyes stinging with tears. "Do you guys have to be right about everything?" she asked in frustration.

Ashley grinned. "Pretty much. Why?"

"The snow's started right on cue. Surely you don't actually control the weather."

Hearing that, Melanie and Maggie rushed over to join them.

"It's going to be beautiful," Melanie promised, stepping up beside her and circling an arm around Jo's waist. "You'll see. By morning it will be like a winter wonderland out there."

"And I'll be trapped in here all by myself," Jo grumbled, awash in an unbecoming and uncommon sea of self-pity. "I'll have nothing to do but think." She shuddered at the prospect. Her thoughts were not all that happy these days. She didn't want to be alone with them.

"We'll rescue you," Ashley promised.

"I'll bring Jessie by and the two of you can go sledding," Melanie suggested, referring to her energetic stepdaughter. "That'll put some color in your cheeks."

"It's cold out there."

"Please," Melanie commented. "Compared to Boston, this is practically tropical. Besides, you used to love sledding."

"When I was eight," Jo muttered.

"Okay, if that doesn't appeal to you, we can all sit here in front of the fire and drink hot chocolate and eat s'mores," Ashley said, her tone soothing, as if she sensed that Jo was about to come unglued on them. "Or Maggie can bake. The whole house will fill up with all these wonderful scents, just the way it did at home when Mom made us cookies on snowy days."

Jo knew they would all be on her doorstep first thing in the morning tomorrow and every day after, unless she put a stop to it right this second. If she ate as many cookies as Maggie was likely to bake, she'd be a blimp by spring.

"Okay, enough," she said firmly. "Don't listen to all my grumbling. You can't turn your lives upside down for me. I appreciate your concern, but I'll be fine. If my thoughts start getting too dark and dreary, I can always go for a walk."

"Of course you can. And there are a few things around this place that need to be taken care of," Ashley said briskly. "Since I was the last one here, I'll make a list of the stuff I never got to do. In fact, I'll make a couple of calls first thing tomorrow and try to line up the right people to come by. You'll just have to be here when they show up."

"I can't afford to spend a fortune on repairs," Jo reminded her. "Until Mike needs me for something, I'm on an unpaid leave of absence. My boss was generous in agreeing to keep the job open for me."

"Generous, my ass," Ashley retorted. "You're the most talented person he has."

Jo grinned at her. "Thanks, big sister, but you're not only biased, you don't know a thing about landscape design."

"But Mike does," Melanie chimed in. "And he says you're good. Don't worry about money, Jo. You'll have all the work you want while you're here. You just have to speak up whenever you're ready."

"And in the meantime, don't worry about the repair bills," Ashley said. "We've pooled money to get this place fixed up. Melanie got the rooms painted and worked on the garden, Maggie made improvements in the kitchen." She shrugged. "I didn't do much, since Josh was teaching me to relax, so I've chipped in for the work that still needs to be done. All the bills will come to me. You'll just need to supervise."

Jo regarded them with bemusement. "Why waste any more money on this place? You all have your own homes now, and Mom hasn't been here since grandmother died except to see you. Why spend a fortune to fix up Rose Cottage?"

"It's not a fortune. We've all agreed Rose Cottage needs to stay in the family, which means it's sensible to keep it in good repair," Ashley said. "And it's yours for as long as you want it."

"Thanks," Jo said, her voice choked. Until she'd actually gotten here, she hadn't realized how much she missed her big sisters. Right this second, it didn't even matter that they were gathered around her in Rose Cottage, the site of her first painful love affair. "You guys are the best." She sniffed and brushed away a traitorous tear.

"Don't start bawling now," Maggie scolded, handing her a tissue. "Or we'll have to stick around till you're finished and we'll wind up being snowed in. Much as you love us right this second, I doubt you're up for a slumber party."

Jo forced a misty-eyed smile. "True." The last thing she wanted was to give her sisters too much time to cross-examine her. "Go, while you can. And call me when you get home, so I won't worry that you've skidded off the road and landed in a ditch."

Relieved by their acquiescence, she stood in the doorway watching until they were out of sight, then sighed heavily. The ground was almost covered with snow already, and there was no sign that it was stopping. It was a little like a winter wonderland she admitted as she stared toward the Chesapeake Bay.

Once, when she'd been starry-eyed and in love, she had thought this would be the place she'd spend the rest of her life. Now it felt more like a beautiful prison.

At least she could leave it when it got to be too much, she reminded herself. If she managed to plaster a cheery smile on her face each time she saw her sisters, eventually they'd relent and let her go home. Until then, she'd lay low and pretend that she'd never heard of Pete Catlett, much less loved him enough to let him break her heart.